Simon & Schuster
Children's Guide to Insects and Spiders

Bumblebee

Previous page: A moth (Olceclostera moresca) camouflaged as a twig
Facing page: Tiger moth, wind scorpion

Simon & Schuster
Children's Guide to Insects and Spiders

JINNY JOHNSON

Simon & Schuster Books for Young Readers

SIMON & SCHUSTER BOOKS FOR YOUNG READERS
An imprint of Simon & Schuster Children's Publishing Division
1230 Avenue of the Americas
New York, New York 10020

SIMON & SCHUSTER BOOKS FOR YOUNG READERS is a trademark of
Simon & Schuster.

This book was conceived, edited, and designed by Marshall Editions
170 Piccadilly, London W1V 9DD

First American Edition, 1996
Printed in Mexico.
10 9 8 7 6 5 4 3 2 1

Consultant: **Dr. Bryan Turner**
Art editor: **Dave Goodman**
Design manager: **Ralph Pitchford**
Managing editor: **Kate Phelps**
Picture editor: **Zilda Tandy**
Copy editor: **Isabella Raeburn**
Editorial director: **Cynthia O'Brien**
Art director: **Branka Surla**
Production: **Janice Storr, Selby Sinton**

The publisher gratefully acknowledges Louis N. Sorkin's expert help and
advice, and thanks him for his contribution to this project.

Contents

6 Foreword

8 What are insects and spiders?

12 **COCKROACHES, EARWIGS,
CRICKETS, GRASSHOPPERS,
AND RELATIVES**

14 Catalog of insects

16 Focus on: Grasshoppers

18 Catalog of insects

20 **MANTIDS, DRAGONFLIES, AND
RELATIVES**

22 Catalog of insects

24 Focus on: Dragonflies

26 Catalog of insects

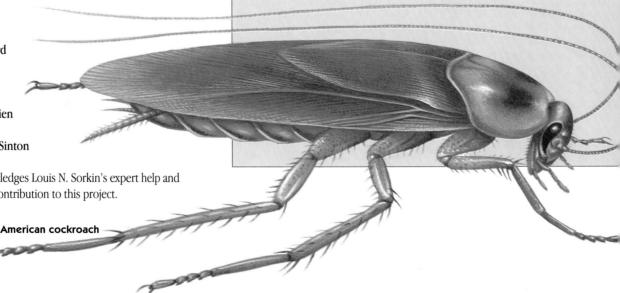

American cockroach

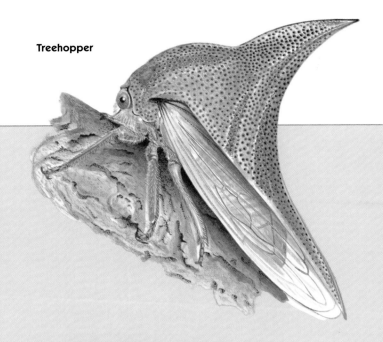

Treehopper

28 BUGS, LICE, AND FLEAS

30 Catalog of insects

32 Focus on: Water bugs

34 Catalog of insects

36 BUTTERFLIES AND MOTHS

38 Catalog of insects

40 Focus on: Sphinx moths

42 Catalog of insects

44 FLIES

46 Catalog of insects

48 Focus on: Mosquitoes

50 Catalog of insects

52 BEETLES

54 Catalog of insects

56 Focus on: Stag beetles

58 Catalog of insects

60 BEES, WASPS, ANTS, AND TERMITES

62 Catalog of insects

64 Focus on: Honeybees

66 Catalog of insects

68 Catalog of insects

70 SPIDERS AND SCORPIONS

72 Catalog of arachnids

74 Focus on: Orb weavers

76 Catalog of arachnids

78 Glossary

80 Index and acknowledgments

Foreword

Did you know that a mosquito's wings beat 500 times a second, that a grasshopper can jump 200 times its own length, that cockroaches are among the most ancient of all insect groups, dating back 350 million years? Insects may be small, but they include some of the most extraordinary of all creatures.

Part of the fascination of insects lies in their adaptability. They live everywhere in the world from deserts to rain forests, from mountains to low-lying swamps. There are even a few insects in Antarctica. The only part of the world that insects have not colonized is the sea.

Insects also have an amazing range of diets. They feed on all parts of plants—leaves, roots, seeds, fruit, and even bark. Some even feed on dead wood and rotting plant material. Many insects are hunters—they catch other creatures to eat. Others, such as fleas and lice, live as parasites, feeding on the blood of other animals. Many insects feed on stored foods such as grain or eat their way through books, glue, and other household items. Spiders are not insects. They belong to a group of invertebrate animals called arachnids, which also includes creatures such as scorpions and ticks.

Stag beetles

Arachnids, too, have extraordinary life-styles—spiders build complex webs in which to trap prey, ticks cling onto and suck the blood of some animals, and a few kinds of scorpions have a sting that can be fatal to humans.

This book includes examples of most of the main groups of insects and arachnids, from the delicate dragonfly with its shimmering veined wings to the glossy stag beetle, and the hairy tarantula spider. The groups are divided into eight chapters. Each chapter includes a general introduction followed by illustrated "catalog" pages of examples. For each example, the scientific name of the family to which it belongs is given, as well as the number of species in that family and the normal size range. The examples chosen are generally typical of their family, both in appearance and behavior. A special "Focus on" feature in each chapter looks at one particular type of insect or spider in more detail, such as grasshoppers, honeybees, and mosquitoes.

Dr. Bryan Turner

What are insects and spiders?

Insects outnumber every other animal on earth. There are about one and a half million known animal species in the world, and about one million of those species are insects. Some experts think that as many as thirty times this number of species are yet to be discovered.

The majority of insects are small—the most common size is about ¼ inch long. Insects have colonized every type of habitat and eat every imaginable type of food. Because they are small, insects can use a vast range of microhabitats that would be unsuitable for larger creatures—hundreds of different species could live in one tree.

Most insects have the same basic structure (below), with three body parts, six legs, two pairs of wings, and a pair of antennae, but there are thousands of variations.

House fly

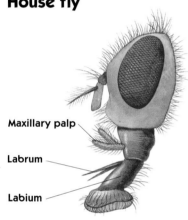

Maxillary palp

Labrum

Labium

Butterfly

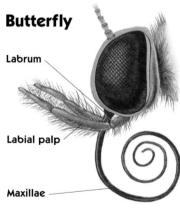

Labrum

Labial palp

Maxillae

The house fly's mouthparts are used for mopping up liquid food—the end of the labium is like a sponge. The ground beetle is a carnivore and has large mandibles adapted for piercing and cutting prey. In butterflies, part of the maxillae forms a tube for sucking up liquid food.

A typical insect

Wings

Compound eye

Thorax

Abdomen

Ocellus

Antenna

Mandible

Labrum

Maxilla and maxillary palp

Coxa

Labium and labial palp

Trochanter

Femur

Spiracle

Ovipositor

Tibia

Claw

Tarsus

Beetle

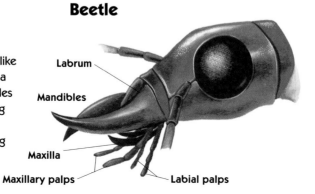

Labrum

Mandibles

Maxilla

Maxillary palps

Labial palps

Mosquito

The mosquito also sucks up its food. All its mouthparts, except the labium, form a needlelike tube called a fascicle.

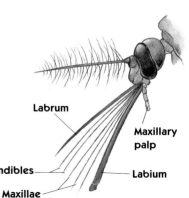

Labrum

Maxillary palp

Mandibles

Labium

Maxillae

Although insects are incredibly varied they can be identified by certain features. An insect's body is divided into three parts—head, thorax, and abdomen. The head carries the eyes, mouthparts, and a pair of sensory antennae, which the insect uses to find out about its surroundings. The mouthparts may be designed for chewing food or for sucking or lapping up liquids.

On the thorax are the insect's three pairs of legs and, usually, two pairs of wings. These wings are made of membrane and are supported by tubular veins which run through them from the base. The membrane may be covered with tiny hairs or scales. In some insects wings do not develop. Worker ants and termites, for example, are wingless.

The abdomen contains the reproductive organs and most of the digestive system. The insect's body is protected by a supporting structure called the exoskeleton to which the muscles are attached.

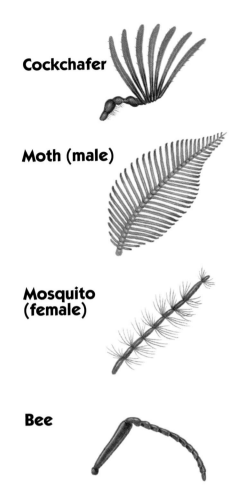

Cockchafer

Moth (male)

Mosquito (female)

Bee

Antennae are sensory structures to help the insect find out more about its surroundings. The structure of some, such as those of the cockchafer, moth, and mosquito are adapted in different ways to increase the surface area for sensory cells. The bee's antennae have a simpler, more robust shape.

INSECTS

WINGLESS
Bristletails (Archaeognatha)
Silverfish (Thysanura)

ADULTS WINGED
(NOT EVERY SPECIES IS WINGED)
Mayflies (Ephemeroptera)
Dragonflies (Odonata)
Rock crawlers (Grylloblattodea)
Stick and leaf insects (Phasmatodea)
Crickets and grasshoppers (Orthoptera)
Mantids (Mantodea)
Cockroaches (Blattodea)
Termites (Isoptera)
Earwigs (Dermaptera)
Web spinners (Embiidina)
Stoneflies (Plecoptera)
Zorapterans (Zoraptera)
Psocids or Bark lice (Pscoptera)
Lice (Phthiraptera)
Bugs, cicadas, and aphids (Hemiptera)
Thrips (Thysanoptera)
Lacewings and ant lions (Neuroptera)
Alderflies and dobson flies (Megaloptera)
Snakeflies (Raphidoptera)
Beetles (Coleoptera)
Twisted-wing parasites (Strepsiptera)
Scorpion flies (Mecoptera)
Fleas (Siphonaptera)
Two-winged flies (Diptera)
Caddisflies (Trichoptera)
Moths and butterflies (Lepidoptera)
Wasps, ants, and bees (Hymenoptera)

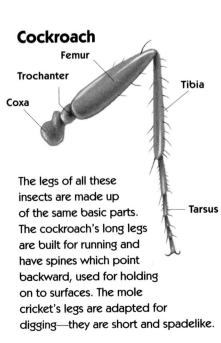

Cockroach

Femur

Trochanter

Tibia

Coxa

Tarsus

The legs of all these insects are made up of the same basic parts. The cockroach's long legs are built for running and have spines which point backward, used for holding on to surfaces. The mole cricket's legs are adapted for digging—they are short and spadelike.

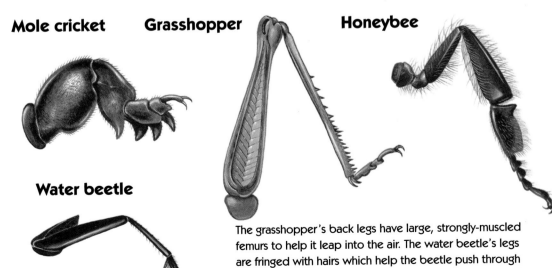

Mole cricket

Grasshopper

Honeybee

Water beetle

The grasshopper's back legs have large, strongly-muscled femurs to help it leap into the air. The water beetle's legs are fringed with hairs which help the beetle push through the water. The honeybee's back legs are adapted for pollen gathering. Pollen sticks to the hairs on the legs and is collected into a special area on the leg called a pollen basket.

Lacewing

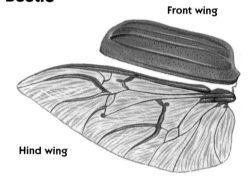

Butterfly

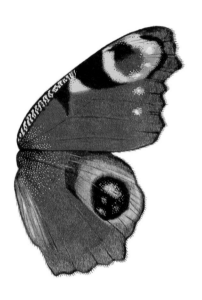

Beetle

Front wing

Hind wing

The lacewing has delicate wings with a large number of cross veins forming a lacy pattern. The beetle wing is more specialized. The front wings are hardened structures, forming protective covers for the folded hind wings. A butterfly's wing is large and covered with minute scales.

One reason insects are so successful is that their basic body structure can be easily adapted to suit different environments and activities. Every insect has the same four pairs of structures on the head. In different species, these structures have been adapted for various purposes, such as sucking, chewing, or biting. The same is true of the leg structure, which can be specialized for jumping, swimming, digging, or running. In some insects, other body parts have been adapted to take on new functions. For example, the stings of bees, ants, and wasps developed from the egg-laying apparatus, and the silk of lacewing larvae comes from the excretory organs.

We are familiar with insects because they eat crops and stored foods, sting and bite us, and carry disease. Yet they do more good than harm. They are by far the most important pollinators of plants, they process dead animals and decaying plants, and provide food for a multitude of other creatures. We obtain products from them, such as silk, honey, wax, and a red dye called cochineal, and we use them to study genetics and evolution.

Life cycle of a bug

  Egg

Juvenile stages

Adult

Life cycle of a beetle

  Egg

Juvenile stages

Pupa

Adult

Insects have a skeleton on the outside of the body so they have to grow in stages, each time molting the old skeleton and growing a larger one to accommodate the increase in size. Most insects lay eggs. Some, such as bugs, then grow through a series of molts, gradually becoming more adultlike. Others, such as beetles, pass through a series of larval stages, quite unlike the adult form, and then pupate. During pupation much of the larval tissue is broken down and used in the formation of adult tissue.

With its brightly colored body this orb weaver is perfectly camouflaged among the flowers of a jungle vine. A flying insect visiting the plant would not see the disguised spider and could be trapped in its sticky web.

A typical spider head

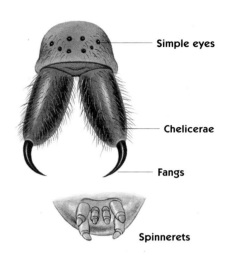

Simple eyes

Chelicerae

Fangs

Spinnerets

A typical spider is shown below and details of the spider's mouthparts and spinnerets (silk-producing organs) are illustrated.

A typical spider

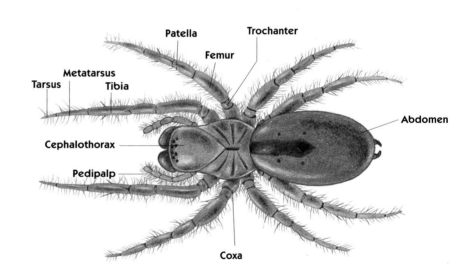

Patella
Trochanter
Femur
Metatarsus
Tarsus
Tibia
Cephalothorax
Pedipalp
Abdomen
Coxa

Arachnids

Although they are often confused with insects, arachnids, which include spiders and scorpions, are a separate group. Like insects, they are adaptable and found all over the world in nearly every kind of habitat. There are at least 75,000 known species of arachnid, of which spiders are the biggest group.

The typical spider's body is divided into two parts. The head and thorax are joined to make one structure called a cephalothorax. This is linked to the abdomen by a narrow waist. The cephalothorax is protected by a tough plate called the carapace.

At the front of the head are the spider's jaws, called chelicerae. Behind these is the mouth. Nearly all spiders have venom glands, but only a few have venomous bites dangerous to humans. Also on the cephalothorax are the pedipalps,

one on each side of the mouth, and four pairs of legs. Males have larger pedipalps than females and they are used in mating. The legs are divided into segments like those of insects and are tipped with two or three claws.

The spider's abdomen contains most of the digestive and reproductive organs. The silk-making organs of spiders are also found in the abdomen.

ARACHNIDS

Scorpions (Scorpiones)
Micro-whip scorpions (Palpigradi)
Whip scorpions (Uropygi)
Short-tailed whip scorpions (Schizomida)
Whip spiders (Amblypygi)
Spiders (Araneae)
Ricinuleids (Ricinulei)
Harvestmen (Opilones)
Ticks and mites (Acari)
Pseudoscorpions (Pseudoscorpiones)
Wind scorpions (Solifugae)

Cockroaches, earwigs, crickets, grasshoppers, and relatives

Among the most adaptable of all creatures, these insects live everywhere from the tops of mountains to city houses.

While these insects are not closely related they share certain features. All of them are strong-jawed, chewing creatures with mobile heads and most have large hind wings. They also share a long ancestry and include some of the most ancient of all groups—cockroaches date back some 350 million years. Most are familiar to humans and some are even unwelcome guests in our homes. Cockroaches, for example, are well-known indoor pests, although most live outdoors, in every kind of habitat from mountains to rain forests.

Earwigs, found in every garden, are also considered pests, since many feed on plants and flowers. Others are welcomed because they catch other pests such as aphids. Like cockroaches, earwigs have flattened bodies, which allow them to crawl into a variety of hiding places. Also common, but less often seen, are the wingless insects known as silverfish, common in kitchens and bathrooms.

Another feature of several of these groups is their ability to conceal themselves from enemies by looking like something else. Among the most extraordinary are walkingsticks, which look like dry twigs, and leaf insects, which resemble living or even dead leaves. Grasshoppers and crickets are often colored to blend in with their surroundings such as leaves, bark, or stones.

This cone-headed katydid may look threatening but in fact feeds on leaves and flowers in the South American rain forest.

Long-horned earwig

FAMILY:	SIZE:	NUMBER OF SPECIES:
Labiduridae	**⅜–1 in long**	**75**

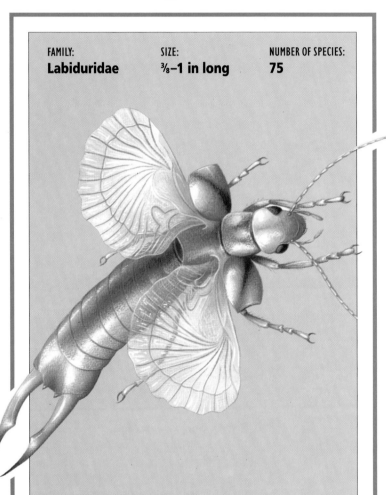

These insects are also known as striped earwigs because of the dark markings on the thorax. Like all earwigs, the long-horned stays hidden during the day and comes out at night to hunt other insects. If attacked, it can squirt out a bad-smelling liquid from special glands on the abdomen. It has large, semicircular back wings which have to be folded many times in order to fit under the smaller, leathery front wings.

Common earwig

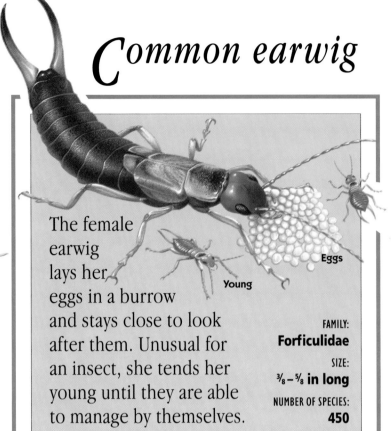

Eggs

Young

The female earwig lays her eggs in a burrow and stays close to look after them. Unusual for an insect, she tends her young until they are able to manage by themselves.

FAMILY:
Forficulidae
SIZE:
⅜ – ⅝ in long
NUMBER OF SPECIES:
450

German cockroach

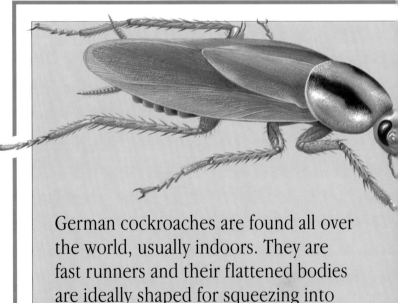

German cockroaches are found all over the world, usually indoors. They are fast runners and their flattened bodies are ideally shaped for squeezing into cracks and under floorboards.

*M*adagascan hissing cockroach

These large, wingless cockroaches make a hissing sound through breathing holes in their abdomen when alarmed.

FAMILY:
Blaberidae

SIZE:
2–3 in long

NUMBER OF SPECIES:
1,000

*A*merican cockroach

Common in buildings, these cockroaches hide by day and feed on anything they can find by night. The female deposits her eggs into a purse-shaped container, which is attached to her body. She leaves this egg case in a dark safe place before the eggs hatch.

FAMILY:
Blattidae

SIZE:
¾–2 in long

NUMBER OF SPECIES:
600

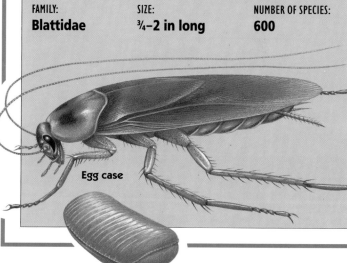

Egg case

FAMILY:
Blattellidae

SIZE:
¼–1 in long

NUMBER OF SPECIES:
1,750

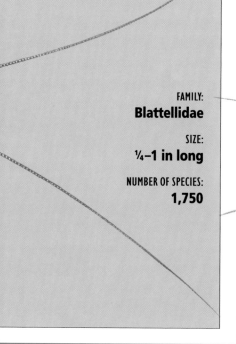

*S*ilverfish

FAMILY:
Lepismatidae

SIZE:
⅓–¾ in long

NUMBER OF SPECIES:
200

Fast-moving, light-shy silverfish usually live in dark corners indoors, where they eat paper, glue, and spilled foods. Its long, tapering body is covered with tiny scales.

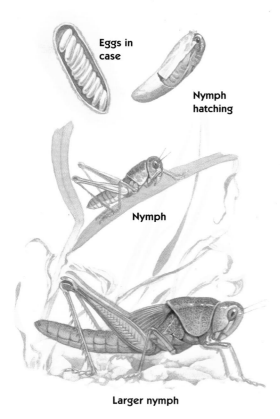

Eggs in case

Nymph hatching

Nymph

Larger nymph

FOCUS ON: *Grasshoppers*

More often heard than seen, grasshoppers are best known for their raspy calls, usually made by males when courting females. Each species of grasshopper has its own particular "song," which only attracts females of the same kind.

There are two main families of grasshoppers: short-horned and long-horned. Short-horned grasshoppers, which include locusts, have short antennae. Long-horned grasshoppers, which include katydids and cone-headed grasshoppers, have extremely long antennae, usually measuring more than the body. Grasshoppers are found all over the world, but the long-horned are more common in tropical areas near the equator.

All grasshoppers have large heads and big eyes—their sight and hearing are excellent. Most have two pairs of wings. The front pair are narrow and leathery and used only as covers for the back wings, not for flight. The broader back wings can be folded away under the front wings when not in use. Most grasshoppers are not very strong fliers and spend their lives on the ground among grass and other plants. If frightened, they escape by leaping into the air and flying a short distance before settling again.

Young grasshoppers
Short-horned grasshoppers lay batches of eggs in the ground. The eggs hatch into tiny young that quickly develop into small versions of adult grasshoppers. These nymphs generally molt five or six times as they grow to adult size.

A mighty jumper
With a spectacular leap into the air, a short-horned grasshopper escapes from danger. Its jump is powered by the large muscles in its back legs and it can leap more than 200 times its own length.

A colorful grasshopper
Some grasshoppers, such as this Australian long-horned species, are extremely brightly patterned.

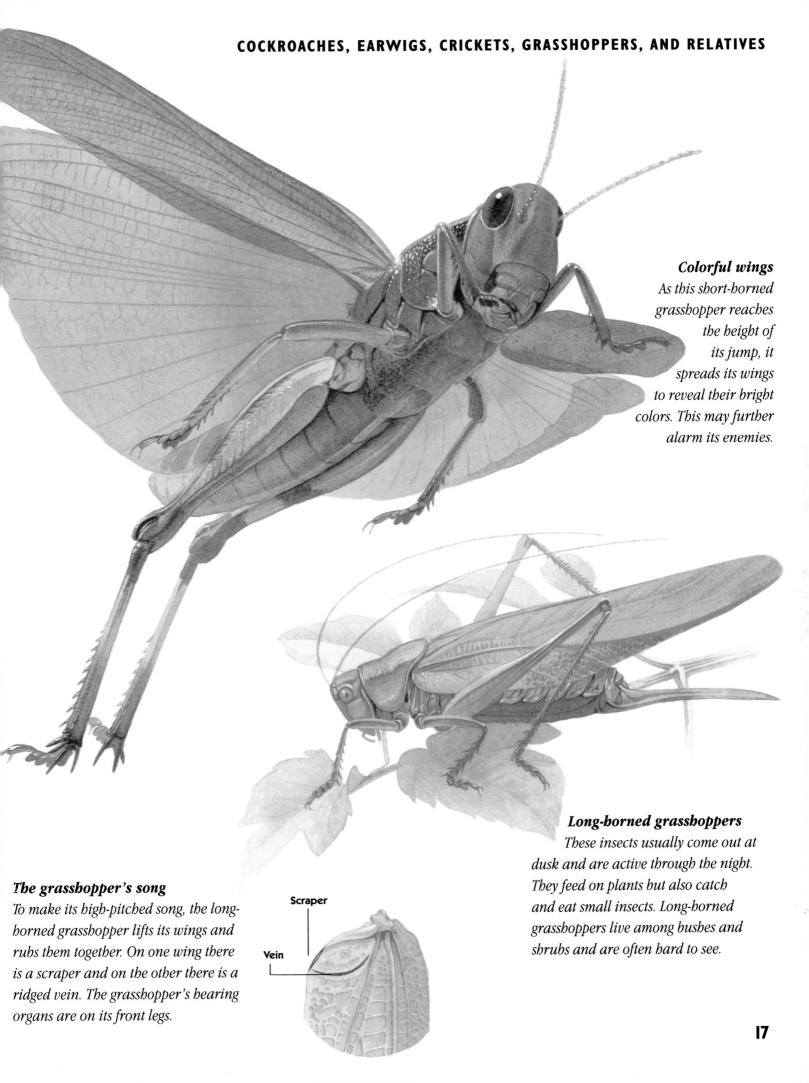

Colorful wings
As this short-horned grasshopper reaches the height of its jump, it spreads its wings to reveal their bright colors. This may further alarm its enemies.

Long-horned grasshoppers
These insects usually come out at dusk and are active through the night. They feed on plants but also catch and eat small insects. Long-horned grasshoppers live among bushes and shrubs and are often hard to see.

The grasshopper's song
To make its high-pitched song, the long-horned grasshopper lifts its wings and rubs them together. On one wing there is a scraper and on the other there is a ridged vein. The grasshopper's hearing organs are on its front legs.

Scraper

Vein

*L*eaf insect

These extraordinary insects are shaped just like the leaves they live on, complete with veins. Even their eggs look like the plant's seeds. Leaf insects live in Asia and Australia.

FAMILY:
Phylliidae

SIZE:
2–4 in long

NUMBER OF SPECIES:
50

*L*ocust

Locusts are among the most damaging of all insects. Huge swarms of locusts swoop down onto crops and feed until there are scarcely any leaves left. A swarm may contain billions of insects.

FAMILY:
Acrididae

SIZE:
½–3 in long

NUMBER OF SPECIES:
9,000

Adult

Nymph

*W*alkingstick

FAMILY:
Phasmatidae

SIZE:
up to 12 in long

NUMBER OF SPECIES:
2,000

With its slender green or brown body, the walkingstick looks so like a leafless twig that it is hard for hungry birds to see. During the day it clings to a plant, with only its long, thin legs swaying gently, as though blown by the breeze. At night the walkingstick moves around, feeding on leaves.

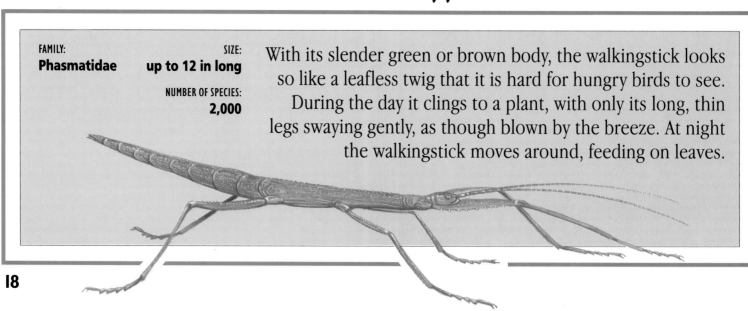

*K*atydid

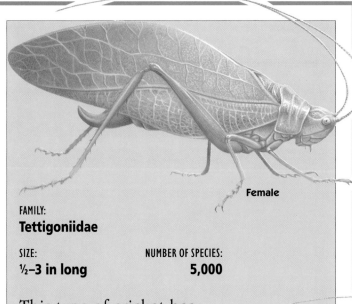

Female

FAMILY:
Tettigoniidae

SIZE:
½–3 in long

NUMBER OF SPECIES:
5,000

This type of cricket has leaflike wings that help it hide among plants. The female has a knifelike ovipositor (egg-laying tube), which it uses to insert eggs into slots that it cuts in the stems of plants.

*T*rue cricket

True crickets "sing" by rubbing together specially ridged and thickened areas of their front wings. They are usually colored green, black, or brown and have broad bodies and tail-like feelers at the end of the abdomen. The female has a pointed ovipositor.

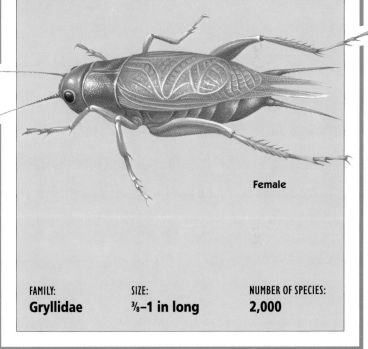

Female

FAMILY:
Gryllidae

SIZE:
⅜–1 in long

NUMBER OF SPECIES:
2,000

*M*ole cricket

FAMILY:
Gryllotalpidae

SIZE:
¾–1½ in long

NUMBER OF SPECIES:
60

Like tiny moles, these crickets live under the ground, where they burrow with their large front legs. A covering of fine hairs protects the body from soil. Plant roots are their main food and they often damage crops and trees. They also catch and eat worms and larvae.

Mantids, dragonflies, and relatives

These miniature hunters range from shimmering dragonflies and mayflies to stealthy mantids.

The insects in this chapter include some of the fiercest predators in the insect world. Mantids are well known for their expert hunting techniques. They are equipped with long front legs, which they extend at lightning speed to grasp their prey. Many are colored to match the leaves or flowers on which they live. This camouflage helps them stay hidden as they lie in wait for victims.

More energetic hunters are the dragonflies, some of the fastest-flying of all insects. They seize their prey in the air or pluck tiny creatures from leaves. Like the slower-flying damselflies and mayflies, dragonflies spend much of their life as aquatic nymphs. Dragonfly and damselfly nymphs are hunters, too. They catch worms, tadpoles, other insects, and even tiny fish in their strong jaws. Most mayfly nymphs filter tiny plants from the water or scrape them from rocks. Less familiar than dragonflies or mayflies are stoneflies. Although they, too, have large, veined wings, their flight is weak and fluttering.

Lacewings, antlions, snakeflies, and mantidflies all belong to the group known as nerve-winged insects or Neuroptera. They have two pairs of delicate, veined wings that can be folded like an arch over the body. Their larvae generally live on land and feed on other small creatures, which they catch in their powerful jaws.

A slender flower mantis sits poised on a leaf, ready to catch any unwary victim that comes too close.

Praying mantis

The powerful front legs of the praying mantis are its hunting tools. They are lined with sharp spines, which help the insect hold onto its struggling prey as it feeds. Females are usually larger than males and sometimes attack or even eat males during mating.

FAMILY:
Mantidae

SIZE:
½–6 in long

NUMBER OF SPECIES:
1,400

Snakefly

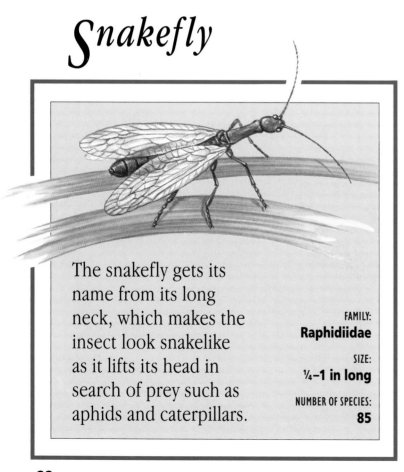

The snakefly gets its name from its long neck, which makes the insect look snakelike as it lifts its head in search of prey such as aphids and caterpillars.

FAMILY:
Raphidiidae

SIZE:
¼–1 in long

NUMBER OF SPECIES:
85

Antlion

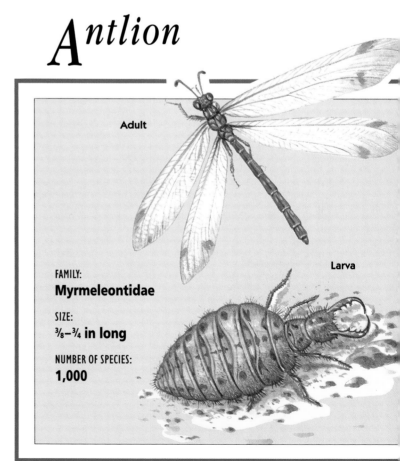

Adult

Larva

FAMILY:
Myrmeleontidae

SIZE:
⅜–¾ in long

NUMBER OF SPECIES:
1,000

*F*lower mantis

Some mantids are colored to match the flowers that they perch on. This helps them stay hidden from both their victims and their enemies.

FAMILY:	SIZE:	NUMBER OF SPECIES:
Mantidae	**½–6 in long**	**1,400**

*G*reen lacewing

Both adult and larval lacewings catch aphids. The larvae suck out the body juices of their victims with special mouthparts.

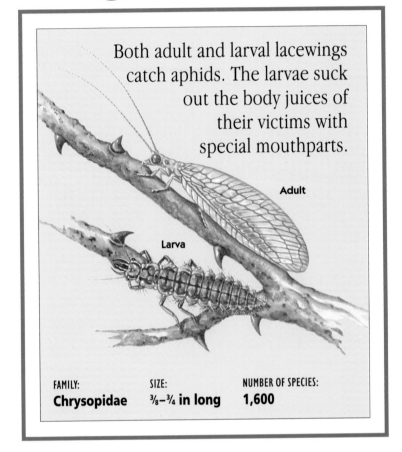

Adult

Larva

FAMILY:	SIZE:	NUMBER OF SPECIES:
Chrysopidae	**⅜–¾ in long**	**1,600**

The adult antlion looks like a dragonfly but has longer antennae with clublike tips. The name antlion comes from the larvae, which are fierce hunters with spiny jaws. The larva digs a pit in sandy soil. When an insect comes near, the antlion tosses soil at it until it loses its footing and falls into the pit.

*M*antisfly

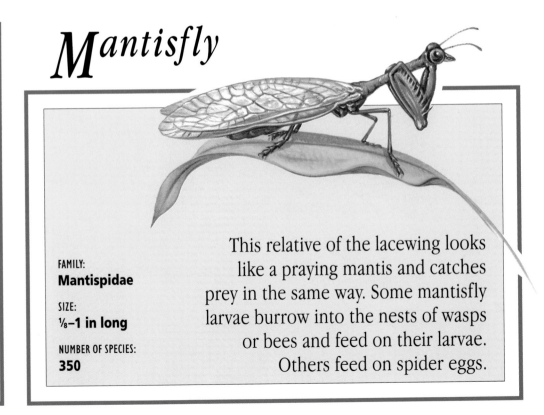

FAMILY:
Mantispidae

SIZE:
⅛–1 in long

NUMBER OF SPECIES:
350

This relative of the lacewing looks like a praying mantis and catches prey in the same way. Some mantisfly larvae burrow into the nests of wasps or bees and feed on their larvae. Others feed on spider eggs.

FOCUS ON: *Dragonflies*

Colorful dragonflies are an eye-catching sight as they dart and swoop in search of prey. They are among the swiftest, most acrobatic of all insects and can chase and catch tiny flies, such as mosquitoes, in midair. They fly backward as well as forward and can reach speeds of as much as 30 miles an hour. Their slender legs are not suited to walking but are used for holding prey or clinging to stems or other supports. When at rest, a dragonfly keeps its wings outstretched, not folded away.

Dragonflies are found all over the world. There are about 5,000 different kinds, ranging from ¾ to 5 inches in length. All have delicately veined wings, strong jaws, and large eyes. They rely on sight to help them find prey.

Usually found near streams, ponds, or lakes, dragonflies lay their eggs in or close to water. The young are called nymphs or naiads. They look quite different from the adults and live in water, catching prey such as tadpoles and even small fish.

Mating
Before mating, the male and female fly in tandem, with the male grasping the female around the neck. Here a dragonfly pair are in the mating position called the wheel.

Dragonfly naiad
The naiad has a long lower lip, tipped with sharp claws, which can shoot forward to grab prey. When not in use, the lip—sometimes known as the mask—is folded up under the head.

Nymph to adult
A fully grown nymph crawls out of the water onto a plant to make its transformation to adult form. The skin splits and the head and thorax come out. Legs and wings follow, and finally the long abdomen emerges. The dragonfly waits by its old skin until its wings and body have strengthened and it is ready to fly away.

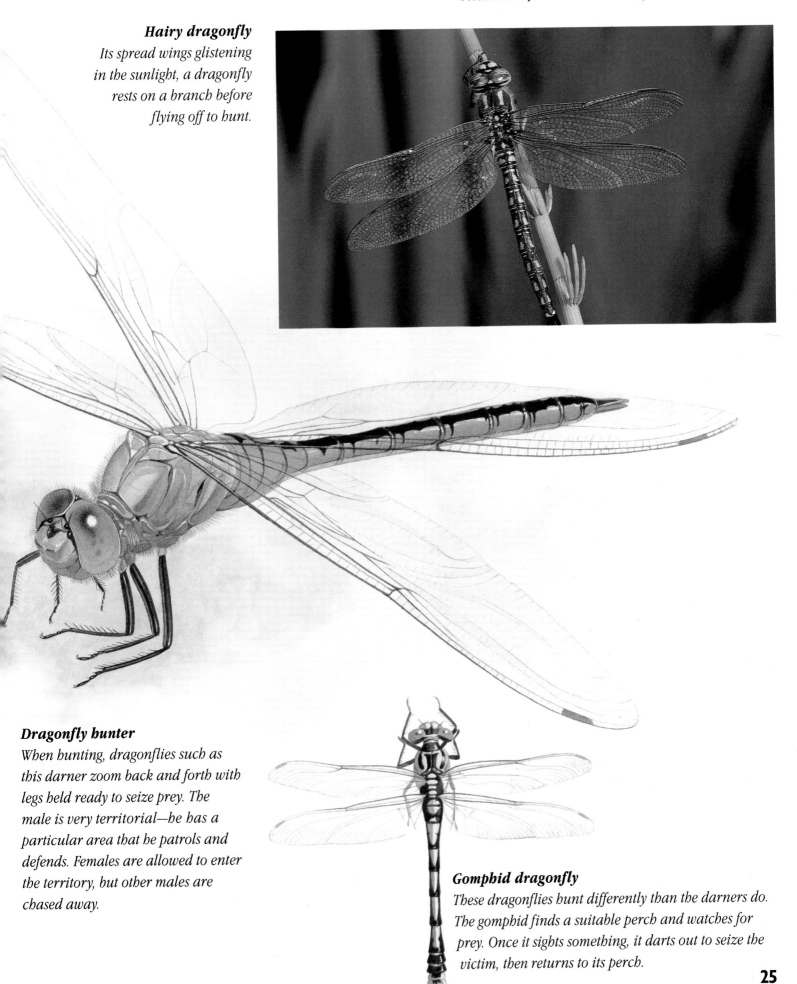

Hairy dragonfly
Its spread wings glistening in the sunlight, a dragonfly rests on a branch before flying off to hunt.

Dragonfly hunter
When hunting, dragonflies such as this darner zoom back and forth with legs held ready to seize prey. The male is very territorial—he has a particular area that he patrols and defends. Females are allowed to enter the territory, but other males are chased away.

Gomphid dragonfly
These dragonflies hunt differently than the darners do. The gomphid finds a suitable perch and watches for prey. Once it sights something, it darts out to seize the victim, then returns to its perch.

25

Skimmer

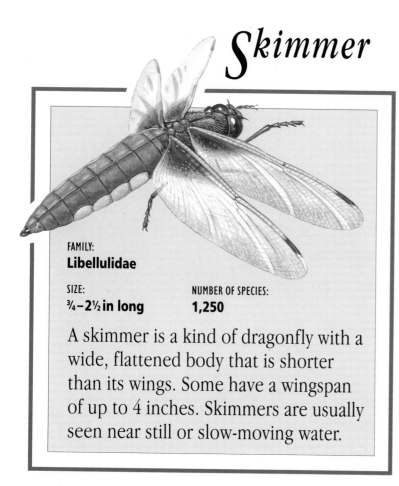

FAMILY:
Libellulidae

SIZE:
¾–2½ in long

NUMBER OF SPECIES:
1,250

A skimmer is a kind of dragonfly with a wide, flattened body that is shorter than its wings. Some have a wingspan of up to 4 inches. Skimmers are usually seen near still or slow-moving water.

Narrow-winged damselfly

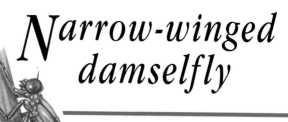

The males of these slender-bodied damselflies are usually brighter in color than the females. Their naiads, like those of all damselflies, live in water and catch small insects to eat.

FAMILY:
Coenagrionidae

SIZE:
1–2 in long

NUMBER OF SPECIES:
1,000

Mayfly

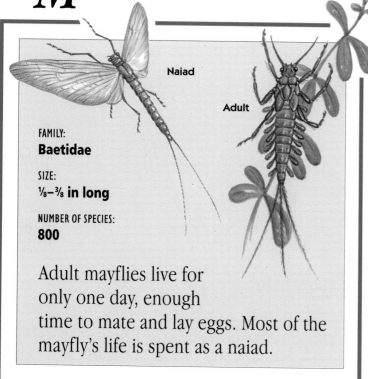

Naiad

Adult

FAMILY:
Baetidae

SIZE:
⅛–⅜ in long

NUMBER OF SPECIES:
800

Adult mayflies live for only one day, enough time to mate and lay eggs. Most of the mayfly's life is spent as a naiad.

Damselfly

These insects are sometimes known as spread-winged damselflies because they hold their wings partly spread out when at rest. They live around ponds and marshes, where they catch insects such as aphids.

FAMILY:
Lestidae

SIZE:
1¼–2 in long

NUMBER OF SPECIES:
200

*B*iddy

FAMILY:
Cordulegastridae

SIZE:
2½–3⅜ in long

NUMBER OF SPECIES:
75

Biddies are large dragonflies often seen around woodland streams, where they hover about a foot above the surface of the water. They are usually brownish in color and have big eyes which meet, or nearly meet, on their broad head, depending on the species. Both head and thorax are covered with fine hairs. Biddy naiads are large and hairy, too. They live underwater at the bottom of streams, where they feed on insects and tadpoles.

*C*ommon stonefly

Stonefly nymphs live in streams, where they feed mostly on plants, although some hunt other insects. They can take in oxygen through their body surface but they also have gills, usually behind the first two pairs of legs, which help them breathe in water. Adult stoneflies are poor fliers and spend much of the day resting on stones with their wings folded flat on their bodies.

FAMILY:
Perlidae

SIZE:
⅜–1⅝ in long

NUMBER OF SPECIES:
350

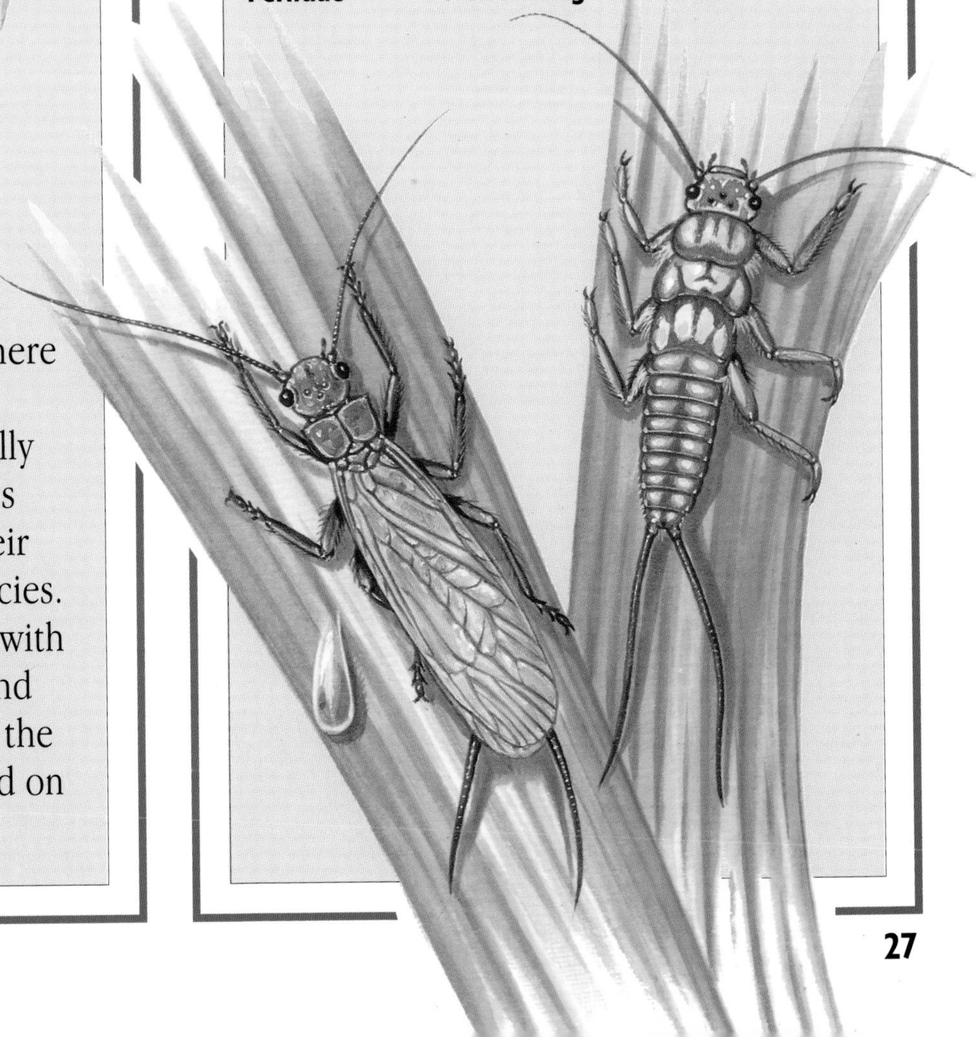

Bugs, lice, and fleas

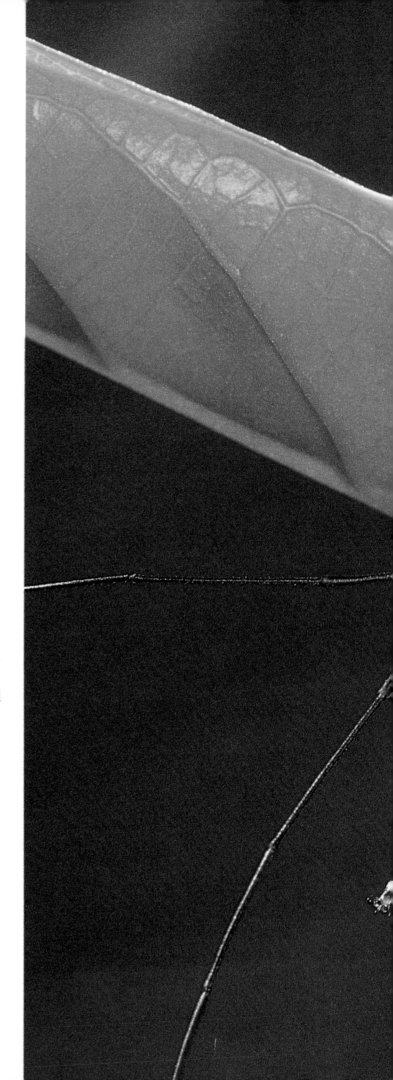

*These insects eat a wide
range of foods, from the juices of
plants to human blood.*

Although the name bug is used for insects generally, it can also describe a particular group of insects. These include a wide variety of species such as assassin bugs, stinkbugs, water boatmen, cicadas, and aphids. All of these insects have special mouthparts for piercing food sources and sucking out the juices. These mouthparts are contained in a beaklike structure. Many bugs feed on plant juices, but some, such as the giant water bug, hunt other creatures. A few types, such as bedbugs, are parasites. This means that they live on other creatures, including humans, feeding on their blood.

Lice and fleas are two other groups of insects that live as parasites. Lice are small, wingless insects, which live on birds and mammals. There are two types of lice: sucking lice and chewing lice. Chewing lice have chewing jaws and feed on the skin, hair, or feathers of their host. Sucking lice have piercing mouthparts and feed on blood; they include two or three species that live on humans.

Fleas, too, pierce the skin of birds and mammals and feed on their blood. Some stay on their host all the time. Others live in the host's home or nest and leap up onto the animal to feed. A flea has a flattened body and no wings. Hairs on the body and rearward projecting spines help it to stay lodged in the fur or feathers of its host.

*The flag-footed bug waves the colorful
flaps on its legs to distract potential
predators away from its body.*

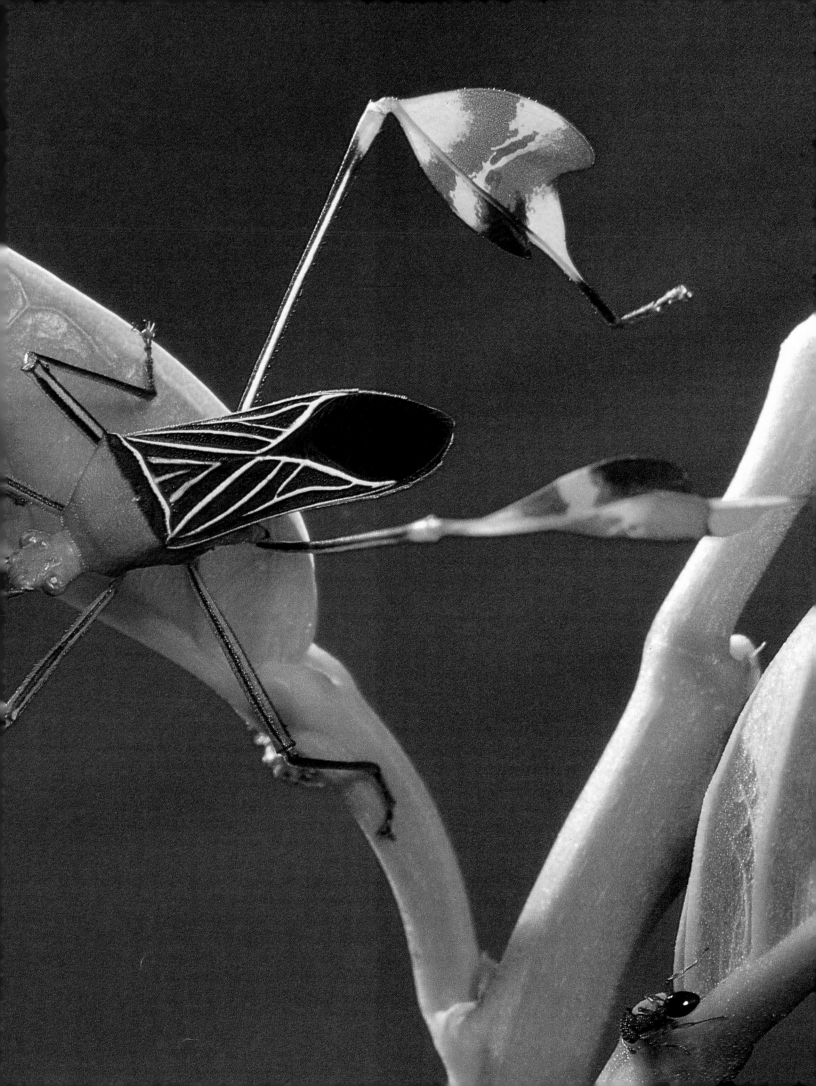

*C*icada

This insect is best known for the shrill, almost constant call made by the males. The sound is made by a pair of structures called tymbals, located on the abdomen, which are vibrated by special muscles. Female cicadas usually lay their eggs in slits they make in tree branches. The nymphs molt several times before reaching adult size.

Adult emerging from shed nymphal skin

FAMILY:	SIZE:	NUMBER OF SPECIES:
Cicadidae	**Up to 5 cm long**	**2,500**

*T*reehopper

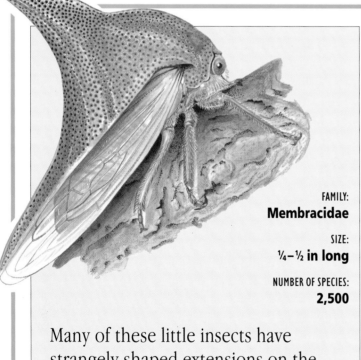

FAMILY:
Membracidae

SIZE:
¼–½ in long

NUMBER OF SPECIES:
2,500

Many of these little insects have strangely shaped extensions on the thorax, which make them look like the thorns of plants. They feed mostly on sap from trees and other plants.

*A*phid

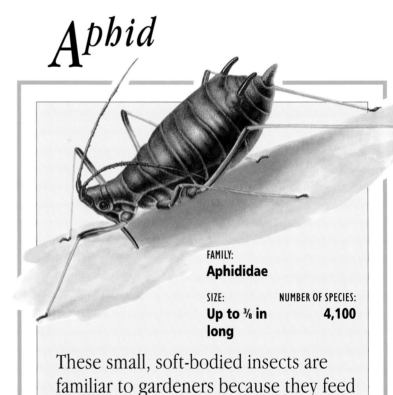

FAMILY:
Aphididae

SIZE:	NUMBER OF SPECIES:
Up to ⅜ in long	**4,100**

These small, soft-bodied insects are familiar to gardeners because they feed on sap from the leaves and stems of plants and can damage them. They reproduce extremely quickly but many are destroyed by insects such as ladybugs and parasitic wasps.

Stinkbug

Stinkbugs get their name from the foul-smelling liquid they squirt at any creature that tries to attack them. The liquid comes from glands on the underside of the stinkbug's body.

FAMILY:
Pentatomidae

SIZE:
¼–¾ in long

NUMBER OF SPECIES:
5,250

Plant bug

The biggest group of true bugs, plant bugs live in every kind of habitat. Most feed on leaves, seeds, and fruit but some hunt insects such as aphids.

FAMILY:
Miridae

SIZE:
⅛–⅜ in long

NUMBER OF SPECIES:
7,000

Froghopper

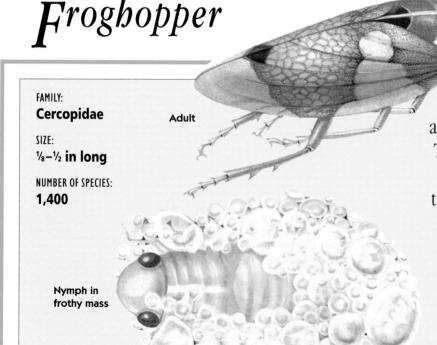

FAMILY:
Cercopidae

Adult

SIZE:
⅛–½ in long

NUMBER OF SPECIES:
1,400

Nymph in frothy mass

Like tiny frogs, froghoppers hop and crawl about on plants as they feed. They lay their eggs on plant stems and when the nymphs hatch they cover themselves with a substance much like saliva. This comes from glands on the abdomen and mixes with air to form a frothy mass. The froth helps to protect the nymphs and hides them from enemies.

31

FOCUS ON: *Water bugs*

There are more than 2,000 different species of water bugs living in ponds, lakes, and streams all over the world. Some, such as pond skaters and water measurers, rarely even get wet. They are so light they can run over the water without breaking the surface and their feet are covered with waterproof hairs. These insects catch other creatures that have fallen into the water and become trapped in the surface film.

Others, such as water boatmen, water bugs, and water scorpions, live beneath the surface and hunt for their food in water. However, they are not adapted to take oxygen from water as fish do, so they have to breathe air. Some simply come to the surface from time to time. Others, such as water scorpions, have long tubes at the end of the body through which they take air from the surface. When water boatmen and backswimmers go underwater, they often swim inside a single bubble of air that surrounds the body like an envelope.

Backswimmer
As their name suggests, backswimmers swim upside down. They move fast, using the back legs as oars. They hunt other insects and small creatures such as tadpoles, seizing their prey with their front legs and stabbing it with their beaks.

Water scorpion
This bug moves slowly through the water searching for prey that it seizes in its powerful front legs. It has beaklike mouthparts and can give humans a painful bite.

Water stick insect
This long slender bug is also a water scorpion but has a much thinner body. Like all water scorpions, it has a long breathing tube at the end of the body. Holding this at the water surface, the bug hangs with its head down, waiting for passing prey in the water.

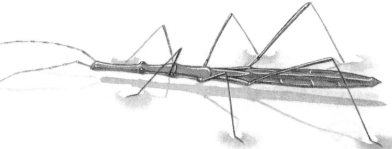

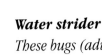

Water strider
These bugs (adult and nymph are shown below) dart over the surface of the water, catching small insects such as mosquito larvae.

Water measurer
The water measurer walks slowly across the surface of the water or on water plants. It often spears food below the surface with its long slender head.

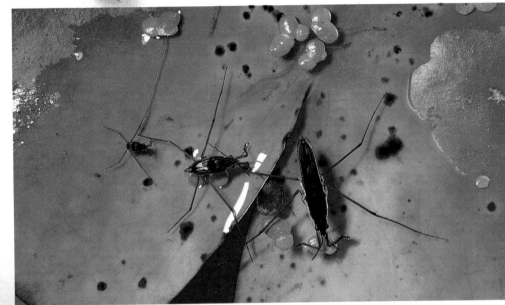

Water boatman
Unlike other water bugs, most water boatmen are not predators but feed on minute plants and algae. They collect their food with their front legs and use the middle and back legs for swimming.

Giant water bug
The largest of the true bugs, giant water bugs can be up to 2½ inches long. Strong swimmers, they paddle with their back and middle legs and use their powerful front legs for catching prey.

33

*B*edbug

FAMILY:
Cimicidae

SIZE:
Up to ¼ in long

NUMBER OF SPECIES:
90

Bedbugs usually stay hidden during the day, then come out at night to feed on the blood of birds and mammals. They do not live on their host but in its home or nest.

*H*ead louse

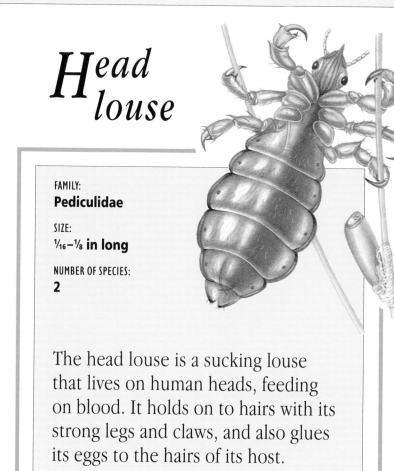

FAMILY:
Pediculidae

SIZE:
¹⁄₁₆–⅛ in long

NUMBER OF SPECIES:
2

The head louse is a sucking louse that lives on human heads, feeding on blood. It holds on to hairs with its strong legs and claws, and also glues its eggs to the hairs of its host.

*A*ssassin bug

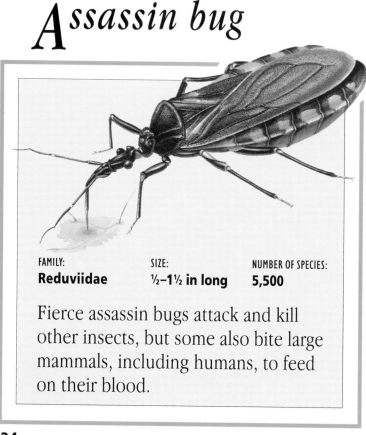

FAMILY:
Reduviidae

SIZE:
½–1½ in long

NUMBER OF SPECIES:
5,500

Fierce assassin bugs attack and kill other insects, but some also bite large mammals, including humans, to feed on their blood.

*C*higoe flea

Like other fleas, chigoes live on the blood of humans or other animals. The flea causes a reaction in the host that causes the skin to grow and engulf the insect.

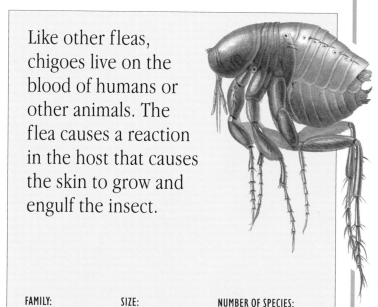

FAMILY:
Tungidae

SIZE:
¹⁄₁₆–¼ in long

NUMBER OF SPECIES:
20

Bark louse

Bark lice are not lice at all but small insects called psocids. There are winged and wingless species. Most live outdoors on or under the bark of trees and bushes and feed on lichen and algae. Others live indoors, feeding on mold or stored food. These psocids are often called booklice.

FAMILY:
Psocidae

SIZE:
1/16–1/4 in long

NUMBER OF SPECIES:
500

Cat flea

FAMILY:
Pulicidae

SIZE:
Up to 1/4 in long

NUMBER OF SPECIES:
200

Like most fleas, the cat flea can jump up to 200 times its length. This helps it leap onto cats to feed on their blood. The spiny combs on the flea's head help to anchor it in the host's fur.

Feather louse

Feather lice are chewing lice and live on a wide range of birds. They have two claws on each leg which they use to cling on to their host's feathers. They feed by chewing on the host's feathers and skin with their jaws.

FAMILY:
Philopteridae

SIZE:
1/16 in long

NUMBER OF SPECIES:
2,700

Butterflies and moths

---

*These beauties of the insect world
pollinate plants as they flit from flower
to flower, feeding on nectar.*

Everywhere in the world that plants grow there are butterflies and moths. Known as the Lepidoptera, this is the second largest group of insects, containing about 150,000 species. Caddisflies look similar to butterflies and moths but are in fact a separate group called Trichoptera.

Butterflies and moths range from tiny creatures a fraction of an inch long to the giant birdwing butterflies of New Guinea, which measure up to 11 inches across with their wings fully spread. Most butterflies and moths are very similar in structure. All have two pairs of wings covered in tiny scales, which are often brilliantly colored. They have large eyes, and most have sucking mouthparts made up of a long, coiled tube called a proboscis through which the butterfly or moth sucks nectar, tree sap, and other liquids. Generally, butterflies are brightly patterned, day-flying creatures while moths are much duller in color and fly at night, but there are many exceptions.

The young butterfly or moth is called a caterpillar. Caterpillars have chewing mouthparts and spend most of their lives feeding on plants and growing at an astonishing rate. When it has reached its full size, a caterpillar stops feeding and becomes a pupa. During this relatively immobile stage, it makes its magical transformation from wingless larva to winged adult.

---

*A brilliantly colored Lycaenid butterfly
settles on a plant and prepares to suck
nectar from its flowers.*

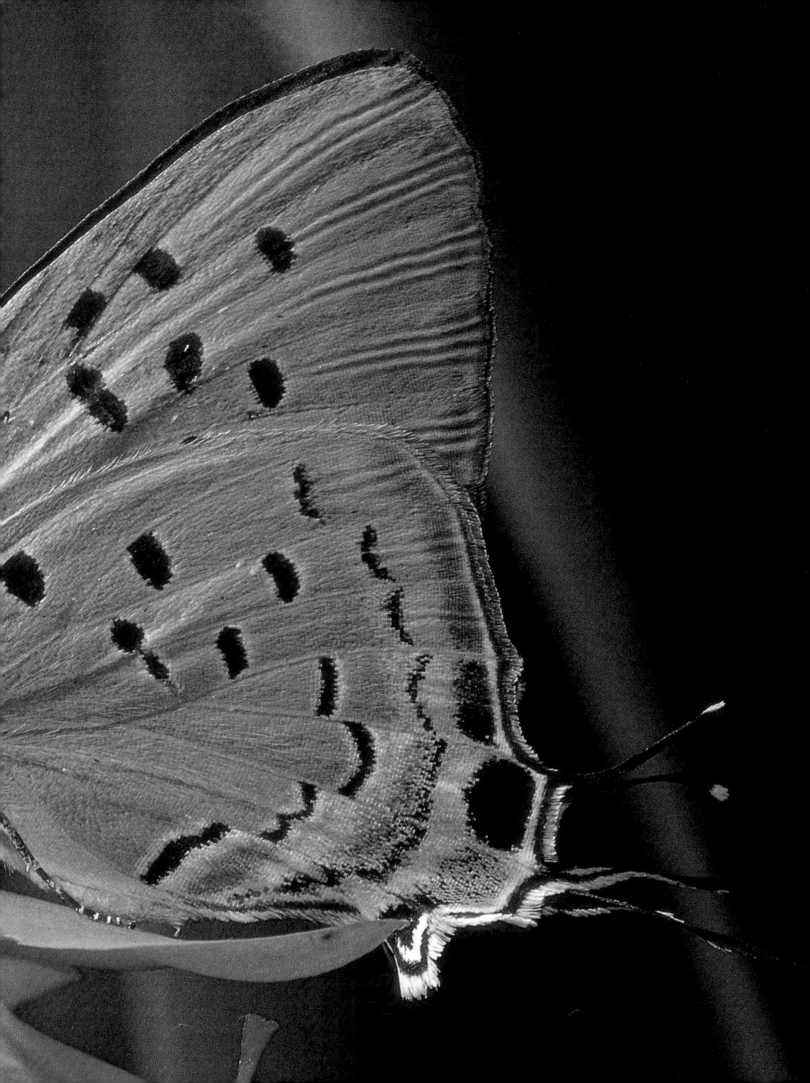

Clothes moth

The caterpillars of the clothes moth feed on hair and feathers in animal nests and on the dried corpses of small mammals and birds. Few creatures, other than some beetle larvae, can digest these difficult foods. Now that humans use animal wool to make clothes the caterpillars often come into our homes to feed on cloth. The adult moths are small and brownish in color, with narrow front wings that are folded neatly over the body when at rest. They usually do not eat anything.

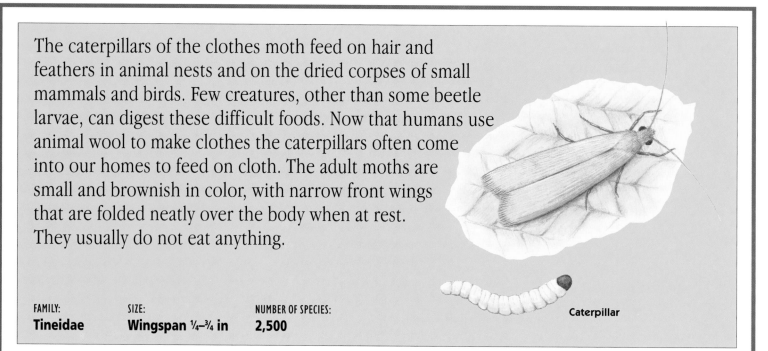

Caterpillar

FAMILY:	SIZE:	NUMBER OF SPECIES:
Tineidae	**Wingspan ¼–¾ in**	**2,500**

Atlas moth

These brightly patterned moths are some of the largest in the world. Most have transparent, scaleless patches on their broad wings.

FAMILY:
Saturniidae

SIZE:
Wingspan 1–6 in

NUMBER OF SPECIES:
1,100

Tiger moth

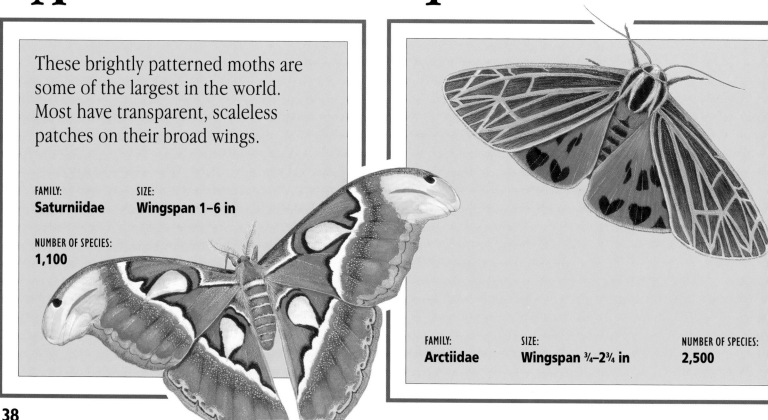

FAMILY:	SIZE:	NUMBER OF SPECIES:
Arctiidae	**Wingspan ¾–2¾ in**	**2,500**

Cotton boll moth

FAMILY:
Noctuidae

SIZE:
Wingspan ½–3 in

NUMBER OF SPECIES:
25,000

This moth belongs to one of the biggest families of moths. Most moths in this family are night-flying and dull in color. The cotton boll caterpillar feeds on cotton seedpods and can damage the plants.

Geometrid moth

Geometrids are slender, weak-flying moths. Their caterpillars are known as inchworms or "loopers" because of the loop shape they make as they move.

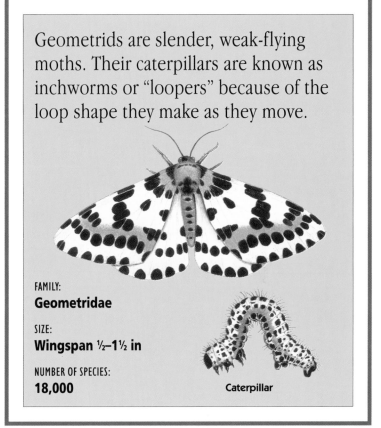

FAMILY:
Geometridae

SIZE:
Wingspan ½–1½ in

NUMBER OF SPECIES:
18,000

Caterpillar

Tiger moths have broad, hairy bodies and boldly patterned wings. The bright spots and stripes of these moths, and of their hairy caterpillars, warn birds and mammals that they are unpleasant to eat. The caterpillars, known as woollybears, feed on plants that are poisonous to vertebrate animals.

Large caddisfly

Caddisflies look similar to moths but have hairs not scales on the body and wings and short lapping mouthparts instead of a proboscis. The caterpillar-like larvae are usually aquatic and live and pupate in cases made of leaves, stones, or twigs.

FAMILY:
Phryganeidae

SIZE:
½–1 in long

NUMBER OF SPECIES:
500

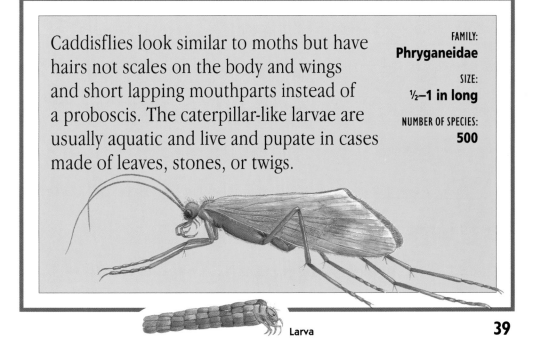

Larva

Focus on: *Sphinx moths*

Of all butterflies and moths, sphinx moths, also called hawkmoths, are some of the most powerful fliers. Their wings beat so fast that they make a whirring noise. The moths can even hover like hummingbirds in front of flowers as they feed.

Like all moths, adult sphinx moths eat liquid food such as plant nectar. They suck up the food with a special kind of tongue called a proboscis. This structure is hollow in the middle, like a drinking straw, and is kept rolled up under the head when not in use. Sphinx moths have the longest tongues of any moths and can feed on nectar at the bottom of long, tubelike flowers.

There are about 1,200 species of sphinx moth, some with wingspans up to 6 inches. Most have large, heavy bodies and long, narrow front wings. Their caterpillars are usually fat and smooth, with a hornlike structure at the end of the abdomen. The caterpillars are sometimes known as hornworms because of this feature.

Bee sphinx moth
A bee sphinx moth plunges its long tongue deep into a flower. With its broad, striped body and the large, clear areas without scales on its wings, this moth looks amazingly like a bee as it hovers over plants. It flies by day, not at night.

White-lined sphinx moth
The white-lined sphinx moth visits flowers at night to feed. Like most moths, it has antennae that are extremely sensitive to smell as well as touch. It can pick up the faintest scents, which helps it to find flowers in the darkness.

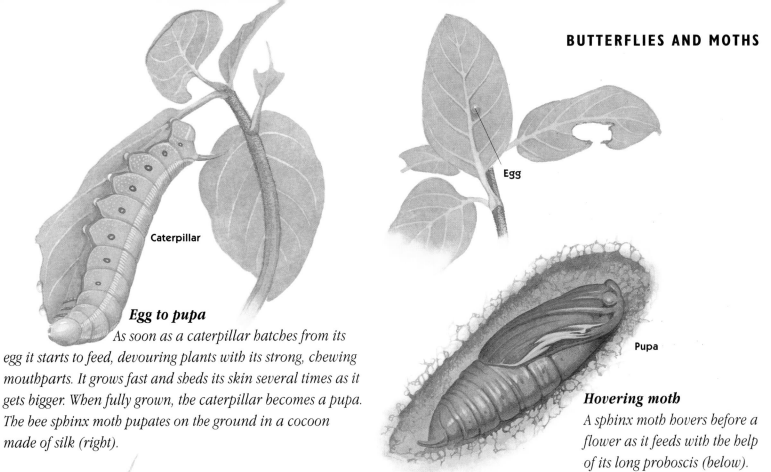

Caterpillar

Egg

Pupa

Egg to pupa

As soon as a caterpillar hatches from its egg it starts to feed, devouring plants with its strong, chewing mouthparts. It grows fast and sheds its skin several times as it gets bigger. When fully grown, the caterpillar becomes a pupa. The bee sphinx moth pupates on the ground in a cocoon made of silk (right).

Hovering moth

A sphinx moth hovers before a flower as it feeds with the help of its long proboscis (below).

Oleander sphinx moth

This is one of the most beautifully patterned of all moths. Its caterpillar has bold eyespots on its body. These can fool a predator into thinking the caterpillar is a much larger creature than it really is.

Poplar sphinx moth

The color and irregular shape of the poplar sphinx moth's wings help it hide on bark during the day. Its caterpillars feed on the leaves of trees such as poplar and willow.

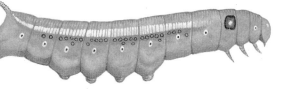

*B*irdwing

FAMILY:
Papilionidae

SIZE:
Wingspan 11 in

NUMBER OF SPECIES:
700

Birdwings, found only in Southeast Asia and northern Australia, are the largest and most spectacular butterflies in the world. Females are bigger than males, but males are more colorful. Birdwings are highly prized by collectors and many are now rare. Adults feed on flower nectar, but caterpillars munch the leaves of plants that are poisonous to most creatures. Both adults and caterpillars are believed to be poisonous to predators such as birds.

Caterpillar

*S*wallowtail

FAMILY:
Papilionidae

SIZE:
Wingspan 2–10 in

NUMBER OF SPECIES:
700

Swallowtails get their name from the tail-like extensions on the back wings. These may help to distract enemies away from the vulnerable head area.

*C*abbage white

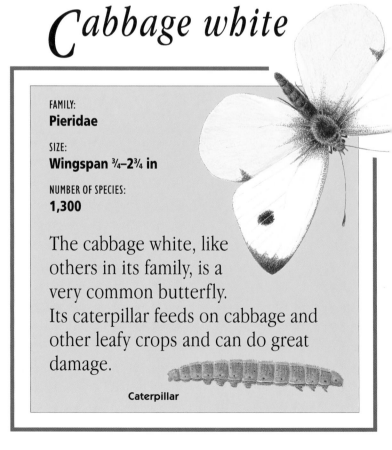

FAMILY:
Pieridae

SIZE:
Wingspan ¾–2¾ in

NUMBER OF SPECIES:
1,300

The cabbage white, like others in its family, is a very common butterfly. Its caterpillar feeds on cabbage and other leafy crops and can do great damage.

Caterpillar

*C*opper

These little butterflies have brightly colored, often iridescent wings. The caterpillars are fat and sluglike in shape. They feed on the leaves of the dock plant.

FAMILY:
Lycaenidae

SIZE:
Wingspan 1–2 in

NUMBER OF SPECIES:
6,000

Caterpillar

*M*onarch

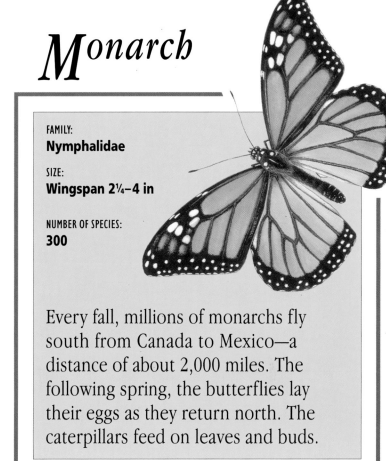

FAMILY:
Nymphalidae

SIZE:
Wingspan 2¼–4 in

NUMBER OF SPECIES:
300

Every fall, millions of monarchs fly south from Canada to Mexico—a distance of about 2,000 miles. The following spring, the butterflies lay their eggs as they return north. The caterpillars feed on leaves and buds.

*M*orpho

Brilliantly colored morpho butterflies live in the rain forests of Central and South America. The beautiful iridescence of their wings is caused by the arrangement of the rows of scales which reflects the light. Only the males are brightly colored; females are much plainer. Like all Nymphalid butterflies, morphos walk on only four legs. The front pair are too small to be used for walking.

Male

FAMILY:
Nymphalidae

SIZE:
Wingspan 1–4½ in

NUMBER OF SPECIES:
3,500

Flies

Buzzing flies may seem irritating to us, but they are important plant pollinators and they eat a lot of waste matter.

One of the largest groups of insects, with more than 90,000 known species, flies are common almost everywhere. One of the few land-based creatures to survive in the Antarctic is a midge, a type of fly. An important feature of flies is that they have only one pair of wings or none. On some, the hind wings are reduced to small, knobbed structures called halteres, which help the fly to balance as it flies. A fly's wings beat fast and it is very agile in the air, hovering and even flying backward as well as forward. Flies usually take liquid food. Many feed on nectar and sap from plants or lap up juices from rotting plant or animal matter. Some, such as mosquitoes and black flies, even suck blood from humans and other animals. Others, such as robber flies, are predators.

Most fly larvae are usually soft, legless creatures, often called maggots, which live in such places as soil, plants, and the bodies of other creatures. The larvae of flies such as mosquitoes live in water and are not maggot-like.

Flies are thought of as dirty and disease-carrying, but they do have their value. They are the second most important pollinators of plants, after bees and wasps. They are a source of food for countless other creatures, including many birds, and their scavenging habits help to get rid of decaying waste, such as dung and carcasses.

A hover fly alights on a flower to feed on nectar. Pollen grains stick to the fly's body and are carried on to the next flower it visits.

Crane fly

With their long thin legs, crane flies look like large mosquitoes. Most adults live only a few days and probably do not eat. The larvae feed mainly on plant roots and rotting plants, although some are predators.

FAMILY:
Tipulidae

SIZE:
¼–2½ in long

NUMBER OF SPECIES:
15,000

Biting midge

These tiny biting midges, also known as punkies, can give a painful bite. Some species bite humans to suck their blood. Others take the body fluids of other insects or eat the insects themselves.

FAMILY:
Ceratopogonidae

SIZE:
¹⁄₁₆–¼ in long

NUMBER OF SPECIES:
2,000

Dance fly

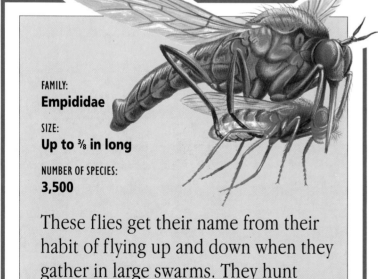

FAMILY:
Empididae

SIZE:
Up to ⅜ in long

NUMBER OF SPECIES:
3,500

These flies get their name from their habit of flying up and down when they gather in large swarms. They hunt smaller insects for food and males sometimes offer an item of prey to attract females at mating time.

Black fly

These flies have stout bodies with a humped back. Males feed on nectar, but most female black flies are bloodsuckers and give vicious bites as they take food from birds and mammals, including humans.

FAMILY:
Simuliidae

SIZE:
Up to ¼ in long

NUMBER OF SPECIES:
1,500

Hover fly

Also known as flower flies, adult hover flies feed on pollen and nectar and are often seen around flowers. They are expert fliers and can hover with ease and even fly backward. Many species are brightly colored and look much like bees or wasps. They do not sting, however. Some hover fly larvae hunt insects such as aphids. Others feed on plants or live in the nests of bees or wasps, where they feed on their larvae.

FAMILY:	SIZE:	NUMBER OF SPECIES:
Syrphidae	**¼–1¼ in long**	**6,000**

Midge

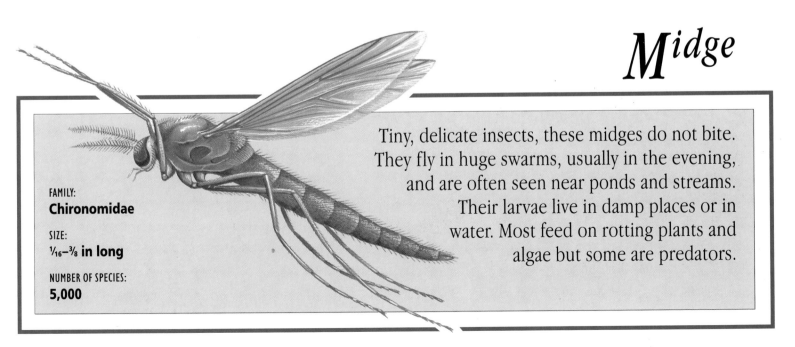

FAMILY:
Chironomidae

SIZE:
¹⁄₁₆–³⁄₈ in long

NUMBER OF SPECIES:
5,000

Tiny, delicate insects, these midges do not bite. They fly in huge swarms, usually in the evening, and are often seen near ponds and streams. Their larvae live in damp places or in water. Most feed on rotting plants and algae but some are predators.

FOCUS ON: *Mosquitoes*

Mosquitoes are usually heard before they are seen. Their wings beat so fast—about 500 beats a second—that the insects make a constant whining sound as they fly. There are about 3,000 different species of these slender, long-legged flies. Although there are more species in warmer areas near the equator, the greatest swarms are found in the far north during the brief Arctic summer.

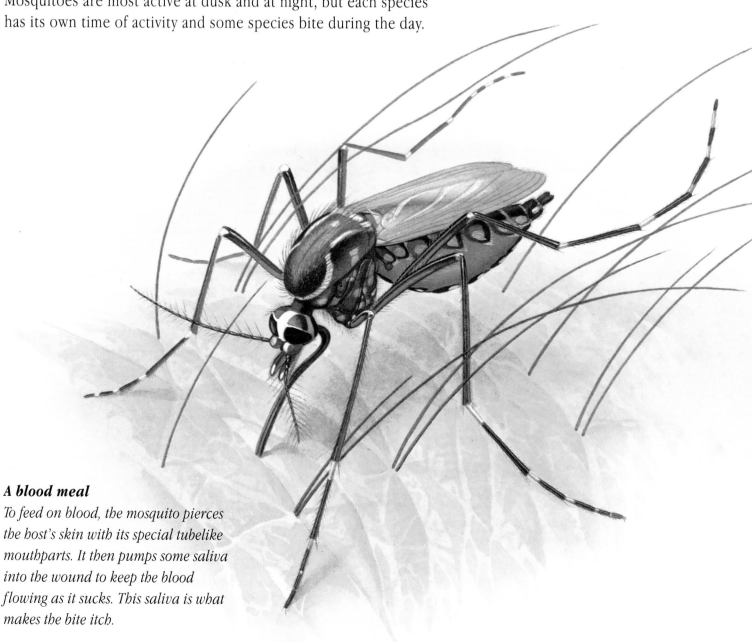

Raft of eggs

Male, and sometimes female, mosquitoes feed on nectar and plant sap. Most females also bite and suck the blood of vertebrate animals—they need the protein-rich food so that they can produce eggs. In one meal the female can take in twice her own weight in blood. Mosquitoes are most active at dusk and at night, but each species has its own time of activity and some species bite during the day.

A blood meal

To feed on blood, the mosquito pierces the host's skin with its special tubelike mouthparts. It then pumps some saliva into the wound to keep the blood flowing as it sucks. This saliva is what makes the bite itch.

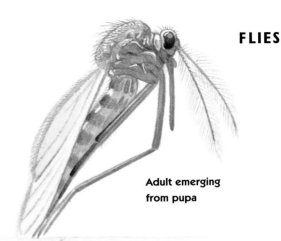

Mosquito life cycle

Most mosquitoes deposit their eggs in water, where they float on the surface, or on aquatic plants. Some species lay single eggs; others lay groups of eggs called rafts. The eggs hatch into aquatic larvae, which feed on particles in the water. The larvae then become pupae and a few days later an adult mosquito emerges from each pupal case.

Adult emerging from pupa

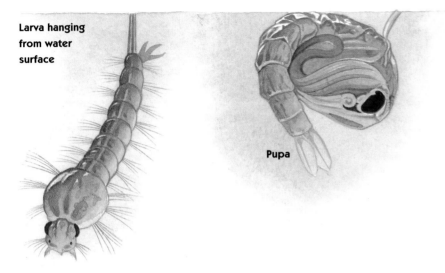

Larva hanging from water surface

Pupa

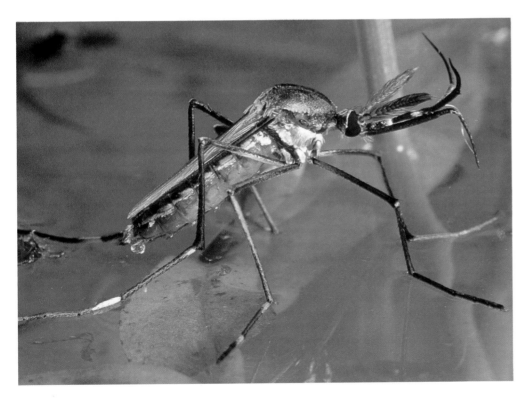

Plant sap eater

Toxorhynchites *(above) is one of the largest of all mosquitoes. Adult females eat plant sap and are not blood feeders. The eggs are laid in places where water gathers, such as tree holes or plants, and the larvae feed on the larvae of other mosquitoes.*

Disease carrier

Certain mosquito species carry tiny parasites in their bodies that cause an illness called malaria. These parasites enter the host's blood as the mosquito bites.

49

Robber fly

A fast-moving hunter, the robber fly chases and catches other insects in the air or pounces on them on the ground. It has strong, bristly legs for seizing its prey. Once it has caught its victim the robber fly sucks out its body fluids with its short, sharp mouthparts. Larvae live in soil or rotting wood, where they feed on the larvae of other insects.

FAMILY:	SIZE:	NUMBER OF SPECIES:
Asilidae	**¼–1¾ in long**	**5,000**

House fly

Found almost everywhere, house flies suck liquids from decaying matter and from fresh fruit and plants.

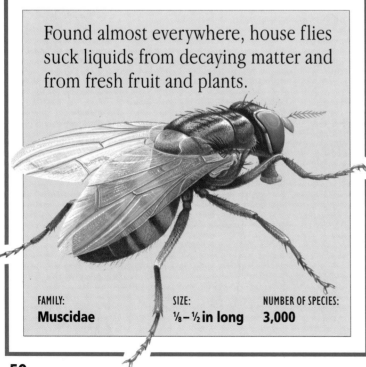

FAMILY:	SIZE:	NUMBER OF SPECIES:
Muscidae	**⅛–½ in long**	**3,000**

Fruit fly

These little flies are common around flowers and overripe fruit. Their larvae feed on plant matter and some are serious pests, causing great damage to fruit trees and other crops.

FAMILY:	SIZE:	NUMBER OF SPECIES:
Tephritidae	**⅛–⅜ in long**	**4,500**

B*low fly*

Adult blow flies feed on pollen and nectar as well as fluids from rotting matter. Many lay their eggs in carrion—the bodies of dead animals—or in dung, so the larvae have a ready food supply.

FAMILY:	SIZE:	NUMBER OF SPECIES:
Calliphoridae	**¼–⅝ in long**	**1,500**

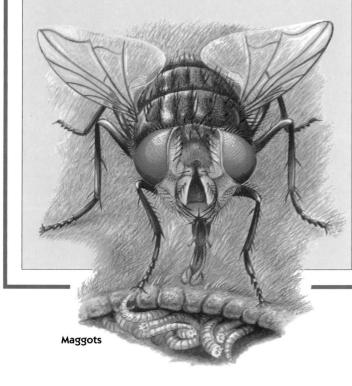

Maggots

H*orse fly*

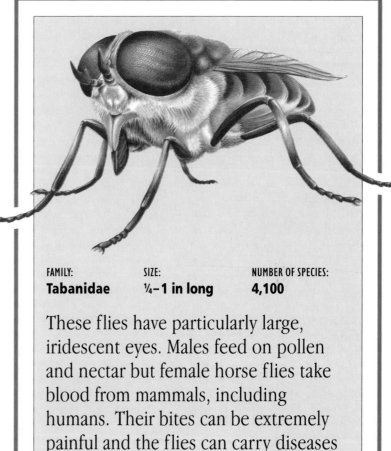

FAMILY:	SIZE:	NUMBER OF SPECIES:
Tabanidae	**¼–1 in long**	**4,100**

These flies have particularly large, iridescent eyes. Males feed on pollen and nectar but female horse flies take blood from mammals, including humans. Their bites can be extremely painful and the flies can carry diseases such as anthrax.

B*ot fly*

Also known as warble flies, bot flies are stout and hairy. Adults do not usually feed. They lay eggs on, or even in, the nostrils of mammals such as horses and deer. The larvae live as parasites, feeding on their host's blood.

FAMILY:	SIZE:	NUMBER OF SPECIES:
Oestridae	**⅜–1 in long**	**160**

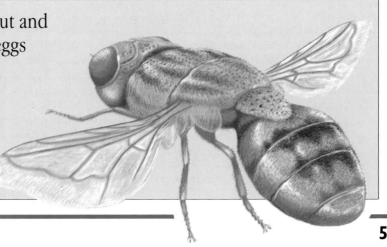

Beetles

Among the most successful of all living creatures, beetles account for 40 percent of known insect species.

Beetles form the largest of all groups of insects. More than a quarter of a million species are known so far— and there are certainly many more yet to be discovered.

Almost every type of habitat from polar lands to rain forests is home to beetles. There is a beetle that can survive in the parched Namib desert in Africa by drinking the dew that condenses on its own body. There are beetles that live in water, and beetles that spend their lives under the ground. Some are barely visible to the eye, while others, such as the goliath and hercules beetles, are the largest of all insects.

Beetles have strong, chewing mouthparts and feed on almost every type of food. Some, such as tiger beetles, hunt ants and other insects. Many eat seeds and the wood of dying trees; others feed on dung or the fur and flesh of dead animals. Where humans provide food in abundance, such as grain stores and timber, wool, and carpet in buildings, beetles take full advantage of them.

Despite their different habits, most beetles have a similar body structure. Their wings are their most characteristic feature. Typically, they have two pairs of wings—the front pair are thick and hard and act as covers for the back wings. When the beetle is at rest its back pair are folded away under the front wings.

The thickened front wings of this gold beetle cover its back and protect the more delicate back wings underneath

Rove beetle

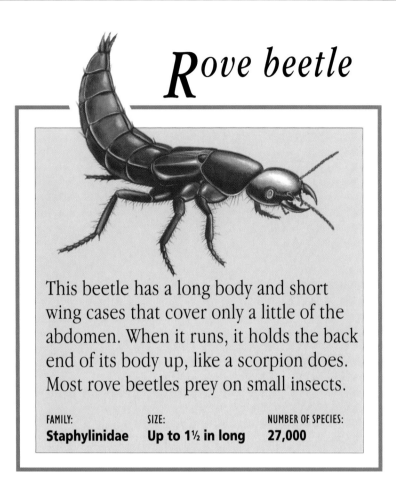

This beetle has a long body and short wing cases that cover only a little of the abdomen. When it runs, it holds the back end of its body up, like a scorpion does. Most rove beetles prey on small insects.

FAMILY:	SIZE:	NUMBER OF SPECIES:
Staphylinidae	**Up to 1½ in long**	**27,000**

Whirligig beetle

Glossy whirligig beetles swim on the surface of ponds and streams, feeding on insects that fall into the water. Their eyes are divided into two parts so that they can see above and below the water surface at the same time.

FAMILY:
Gyrinidae

SIZE:
⅛–⅝ in long

NUMBER OF SPECIES:
750

Goliath beetle

One of the largest and heaviest of all insects is the goliath beetle, found in Africa. Males are the giants; females are smaller and less brightly patterned. These beetles have strong front legs and are good climbers. They clamber up into trees in search of sap and soft fruit to eat.

Male

FAMILY:	SIZE:	NUMBER OF SPECIES:
Scarabaeidae	**¾–5 in long**	**20,000**

Tiger beetle

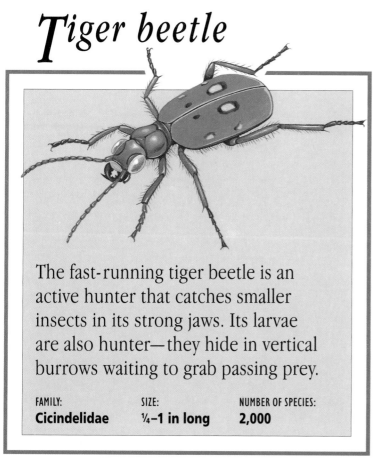

The fast-running tiger beetle is an active hunter that catches smaller insects in its strong jaws. Its larvae are also hunter—they hide in vertical burrows waiting to grab passing prey.

FAMILY:
Cicindelidae

SIZE:
¼–1 in long

NUMBER OF SPECIES:
2,000

Diving beetle

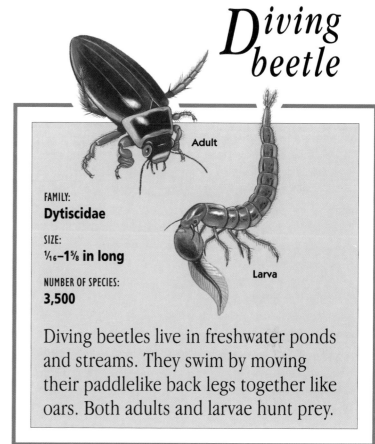

Adult

FAMILY:
Dytiscidae

SIZE:
¹⁄₁₆–1⅝ in long

NUMBER OF SPECIES:
3,500

Larva

Diving beetles live in freshwater ponds and streams. They swim by moving their paddlelike back legs together like oars. Both adults and larvae hunt prey.

Carrion beetle

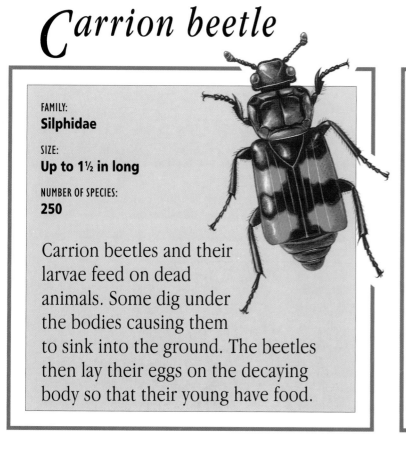

FAMILY:
Silphidae

SIZE:
Up to 1½ in long

NUMBER OF SPECIES:
250

Carrion beetles and their larvae feed on dead animals. Some dig under the bodies causing them to sink into the ground. The beetles then lay their eggs on the decaying body so that their young have food.

Jewel beetle

With their gleaming metallic colors, jewel beetles deserve their name. They live in woodland, usually in tropical areas, where adults feed on nectar and leaves. The larvae bore into dead or living wood as they eat and cause much damage.

FAMILY:
Buprestidae

SIZE:
¾–2½ in long

NUMBER OF SPECIES:
14,000

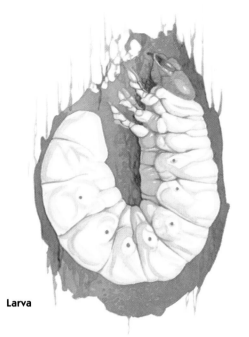

Larva

Focus on: *Stag beetles*

With their large heads and massive jaws, male stag beetles are among the most spectacular of all insects. But despite their fearsome appearance, these insects are harmless and feed mostly on tree sap and other liquids. There are about 1,250 species, some up to 4 inches long. Most are black or brownish in color. Stag beetles usually live in woodland and are particularly common in tropical areas .

The jaws of the males are branched like the antlers of a stag and, like stags, these beetles battle with one another to win females. They rarely fight to the death—their jaw muscles are too weak to give any power to a bite—but they sometimes damage each other's wing cases. The beetle with the biggest jaws usually wins the contest.

Females lay their eggs in cracks in logs or dead tree stumps. The larvae feed on the juices of the rotting wood.

Larva and pupa

Stag beetle eggs hatch into wormlike larvae called grubs. As a larva grows, it molts several times—it sheds its skin to allow for the increase in body size. When the larva is full grown, it becomes a pupa—the stage during which the larva changes into an adult beetle.

Pupa

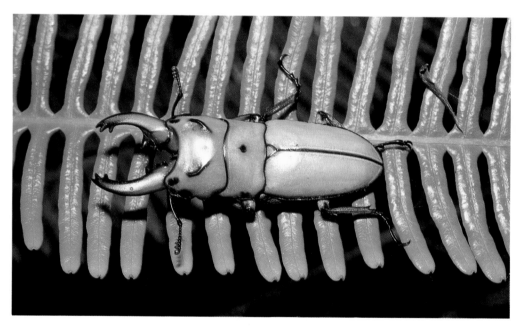

Jungle beetle

A magnificent tropical stag beetle rests on a fern frond in a Malaysian rain forest.

The female stag beetle

The smaller female stag beetle does not have the large jaws of the male. However, she can give a much more powerful nip. The male's mighty jaws are almost useless for feeding or biting.

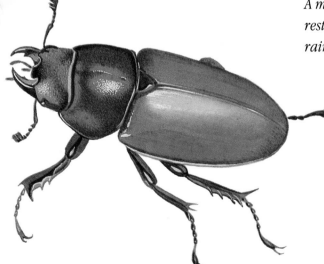

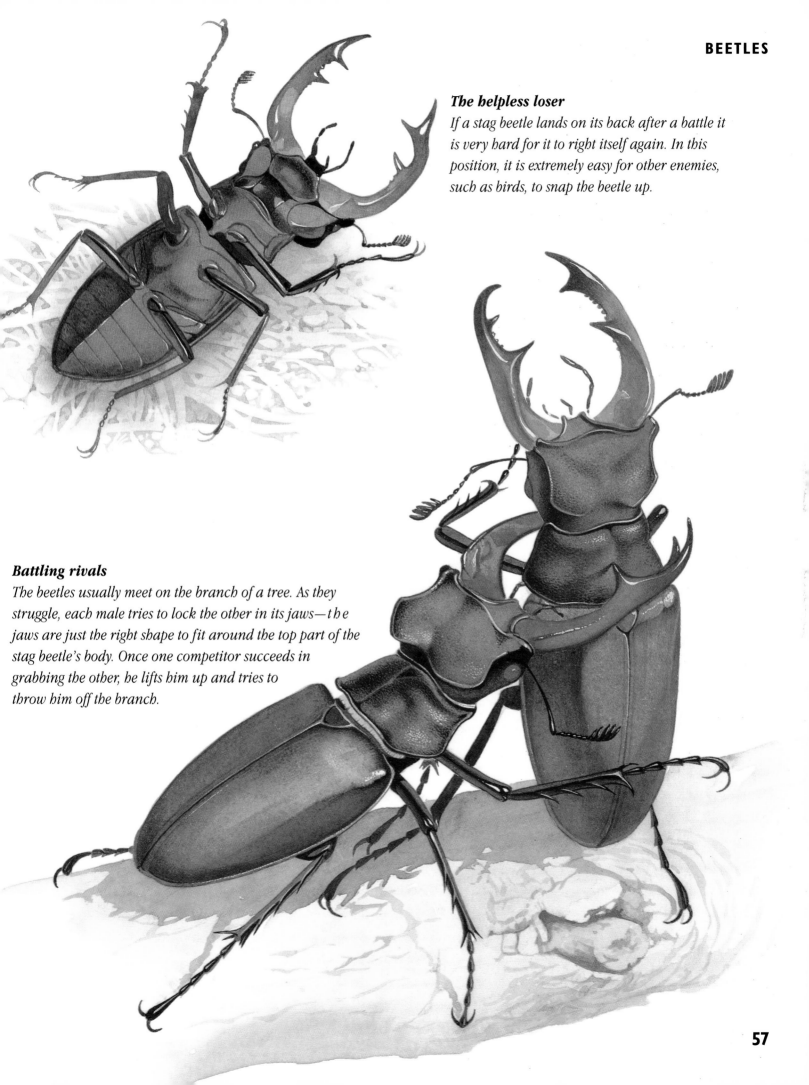

The helpless loser

If a stag beetle lands on its back after a battle it is very hard for it to right itself again. In this position, it is extremely easy for other enemies, such as birds, to snap the beetle up.

Battling rivals

The beetles usually meet on the branch of a tree. As they struggle, each male tries to lock the other in its jaws—the jaws are just the right shape to fit around the top part of the stag beetle's body. Once one competitor succeeds in grabbing the other, he lifts him up and tries to throw him off the branch.

Darkling beetle

FAMILY:
Tenebrionidae

SIZE:
¾–1¾ in long

NUMBER OF SPECIES:
15,000

Common in dry areas, where they lurk under stones, darkling beetles are usually slow-moving insects that come out at night. They are scavengers and eat many foods, including plants, insect larvae, and stored grain.

Longhorn beetle

This beetle has extremely long antennae—up to three times the length of its body. Adults feed on plants, many on flowers and pollen. They lay their eggs in crevices in living trees or logs and their larvae tunnel into the wood as they feed.

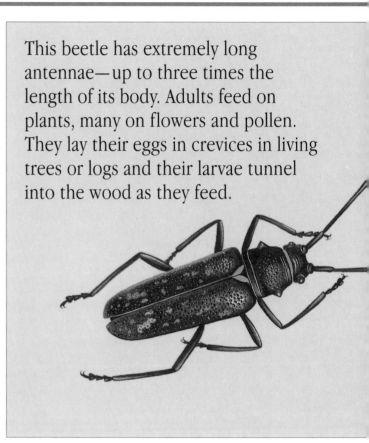

Boll weevil

FAMILY:
Curculionidae

SIZE:
¹⁄₁₆–1⅝ in long

NUMBER OF SPECIES:
40,000

This weevil belongs to the snout beetle family. All eat plants and can cause serious damage. The boll weevil uses its long snout to bore into the seedpods—called bolls—and buds of cotton plants. Females also lay their eggs in holes made in seedpods.

Click beetle

The clicking sound made as they leap into the air to right themselves gives these beetles their name. Their larvae are pests known as wireworms.

FAMILY:
Elateridae

SIZE:
Up to 2½ in long

NUMBER OF SPECIES:
8,500

L*adybug*

FAMILY:
Cerambycidae

SIZE:
Up to 7 in long, including antennae

NUMBER OF SPECIES:
25,000

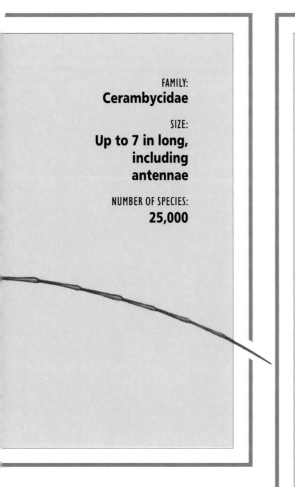

FAMILY:
Coccinellidae

SIZE:
Up to ⅜ in long

NUMBER OF SPECIES:
5,000

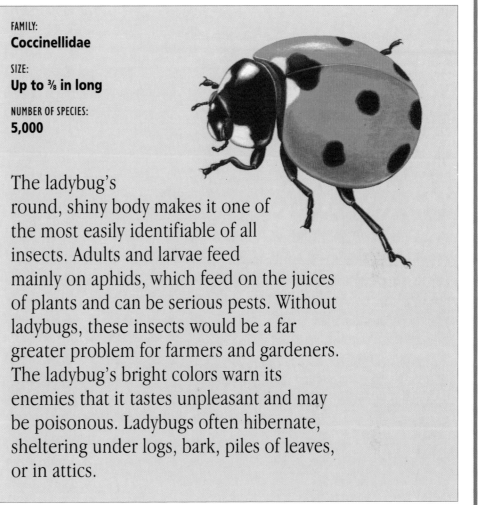

The ladybug's round, shiny body makes it one of the most easily identifiable of all insects. Adults and larvae feed mainly on aphids, which feed on the juices of plants and can be serious pests. Without ladybugs, these insects would be a far greater problem for farmers and gardeners. The ladybug's bright colors warn its enemies that it tastes unpleasant and may be poisonous. Ladybugs often hibernate, sheltering under logs, bark, piles of leaves, or in attics.

F*irefly*

Fireflies can produce a yellowish green light in a special area at the end of the abdomen. Each species of firefly flashes its light in a particular pattern to attract mates. Male fireflies have wings, but females are often wingless and look like larvae.

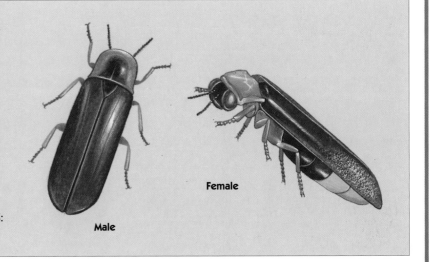

Female

Male

FAMILY:
Lampyridae

SIZE:
Up to 1 in long

NUMBER OF SPECIES:
2,000

Bees, wasps, ants, and termites

Many of these insects live in well-organized colonies containing thousands of individuals, each with its own tasks.

Bees, wasps, and ants belong to a large group of insects known as the Hymenoptera, which includes some of the most fascinating of all insects. Although they vary greatly in appearance, most have a definite "waist" at the front of the abdomen. They have chewing mouthparts and tonguelike structures for sucking liquids such as nectar from flowers. Hymenopterans that do have wings have two pairs but many worker ants are wingless. The most primitive members of the group are sawflies, which do not have the distinctive "waist."

While most hymenopterans lead solitary lives, ants and some bees and wasps live in complex social colonies. Typically, a colony is headed by a queen who is the only female to mate and lay eggs. Other females are workers who build the nest, gather food, and care for young but do not usually lay eggs. There are generally far fewer males in a colony. They do not work and are present only at certain times of the year to mate with new queens.

Termites have a similar social system, although they are not related to bees, wasps, and ants. Small insects with biting mouthparts, termites live in huge colonies in nests made in wood, soil, or trees, or in specially built mounds. Unlike certain bees and wasps, they lay their eggs in special chambers in the nest, not in individual cells.

The giant hornet is a type of wasp. It feeds on plant nectar and also catches other insects to eat and to feed to its larvae.

*A*rmy ant

Unlike other ants, army ants do not build permanent nests. They march in search of prey, overpowering insects or other small creatures in their way. Periodically they stop to produce eggs and remain in one place until the young have developed. The worker ants link their bodies together, making a temporary nest called a bivouac to protect the queen and young.

FAMILY:
Formicidae

SIZE:
¹⁄₁₆–1 in

NUMBER OF SPECIES:
8,800

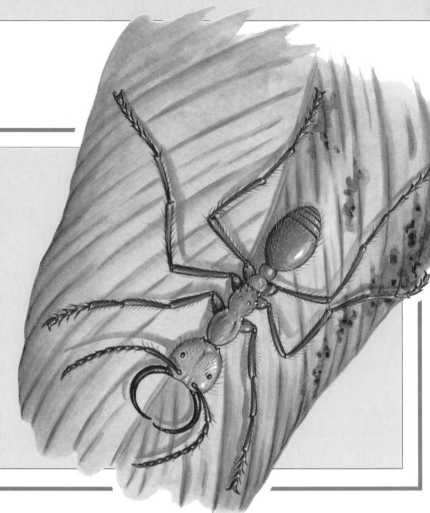

*F*ire ant

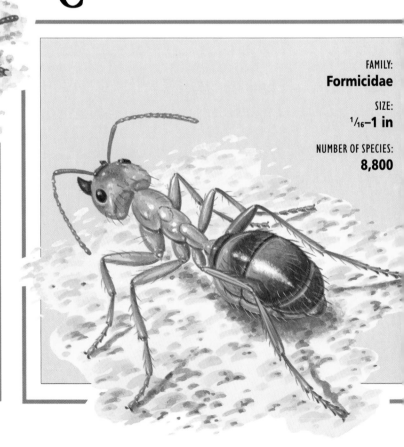

As its name suggests, the fire ant has a powerful bite and sting. It hunts other insects but also eats seeds, fruit, and flowers.

FAMILY:
Formicidae

SIZE:
¹⁄₁₆–1 in

NUMBER OF SPECIES:
8,800

*C*arpenter ant

FAMILY:
Formicidae

SIZE:
¹⁄₁₆–1 in

NUMBER OF SPECIES:
8,800

*S*nouted termite

Only the soldiers of these termite species have long snouts. They use their snouts to spray sticky, bad-smelling fluid at ants and other enemies.

FAMILY:
Termitidae

SIZE:
Up to 1 in long

Soldier

NUMBER OF SPECIES:
1,650

*D*rywood termite

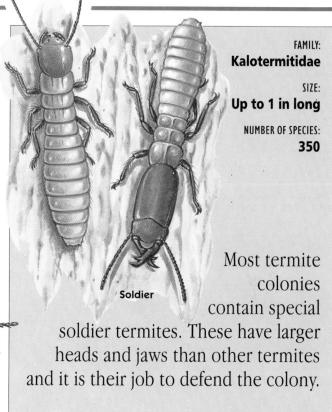

FAMILY:
Kalotermitidae

SIZE:
Up to 1 in long

NUMBER OF SPECIES:
350

Soldier

Most termite colonies contain special soldier termites. These have larger heads and jaws than other termites and it is their job to defend the colony.

Colonies of carpenter ants make their nests in wooden buildings or rotting tree trunks. As with all ants, most members of a colony are female. The queen ant lays all of the eggs. The workers are also female but do not lay eggs. They do the work of the colony, gathering food and looking after the nest and young.

*L*eafcutting ant

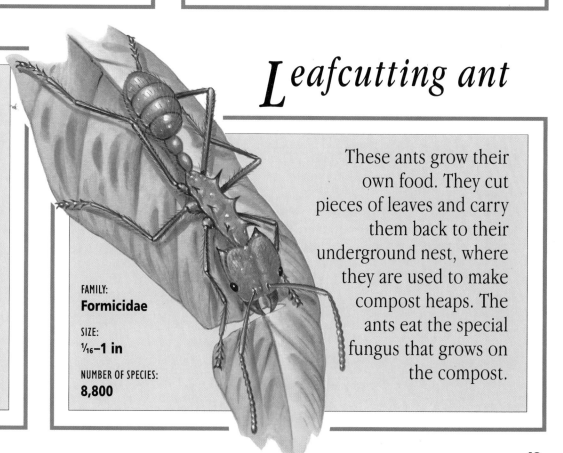

FAMILY:
Formicidae

SIZE:
¹⁄₁₆–1 in

NUMBER OF SPECIES:
8,800

These ants grow their own food. They cut pieces of leaves and carry them back to their underground nest, where they are used to make compost heaps. The ants eat the special fungus that grows on the compost.

FOCUS ON: *Honeybees*

Of all the many types of bees, honeybees are probably the best known. They pollinate countless food crops and produce millions of dollars' worth of honey and wax every year.

Many bees lead solitary lives, but honeybees live in huge colonies of thousands of bees, with a complex social organization. Each colony has a queen. The queen bee is larger than the other bees and lays all the eggs of the colony. Most of the members of the colony are female workers. They care for the young, build and repair the nest, and gather food, but do not lay eggs. At only certain times of the year are there male bees in the colony. They do no work and are there only to mate with new queens. The nest is made in a hollow tree or in a hive provided by a beekeeper and consists of sheets of hexagonal—six-sided—cells. These cells contain eggs and young as well as food stores of pollen and honey.

Worker bees

A worker honeybee lives only about six weeks. For the first week of her adult life she cares for the eggs and larvae of the colony. Then she helps to build cells and maintain the nest. Finally, she becomes a food gatherer, bringing nectar and pollen back to the nest.

The royal cell

Special cells for future queens hang down from the edge of the comb. The larvae in queen cells are fed on royal jelly—a protein-rich substance from glands on the heads of workers. Worker larvae are only given royal jelly for a few days and are then fed on pollen and nectar.

Busy bees

Worker bees always have plenty to do in the nest. When a bee returns from a foraging trip laden with pollen and nectar (left), the other bees gather around to collect the food stores. Workers also make the nest cells, building them from wax produced in glands on the underside of the bee's abdomen.

Equipped for work

All the tools needed by a worker bee are on her own body. On each front leg there are long hairs used to remove pollen from the body and a special notch for cleaning the antennae. On the middle legs there are fringes of hair for removing pollen from the forelegs and a spike for taking wax from glands in the abdomen. On each hind leg there is a pollen basket—a special area lined with hairs where pollen is carried.

*Y*ellow jacket wasp

Adult yellow jackets feed mainly on nectar and other sweet things such as ripe fruit. They do catch other insects, however, to feed to their young. Yellow jackets are well known for their sting. The pointed sting is at the end of the body and is linked to a bag of poison. The yellow jacket uses its sting to kill prey and to defend itself against enemies—including humans.

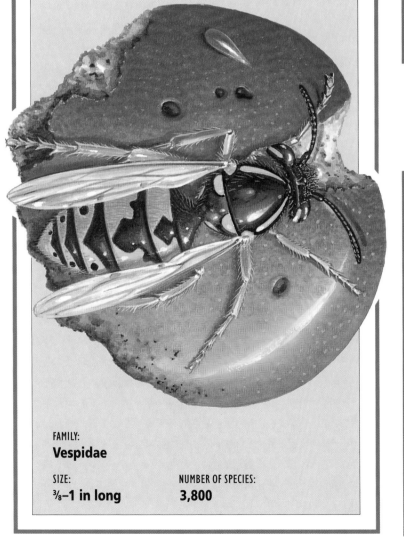

FAMILY:
Vespidae

SIZE:
³⁄₈–1 in long

NUMBER OF SPECIES:
3,800

*M*ud dauber

The female mud dauber wasp makes a nest of damp mud. Into each cell she puts an egg and paralyzed spiders for her young to eat when it hatches.

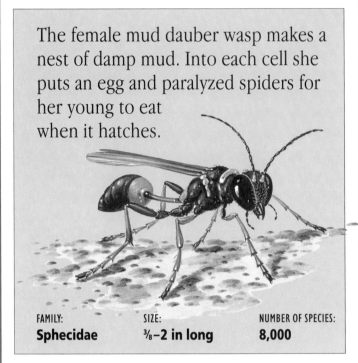

FAMILY:
Sphecidae

SIZE:
³⁄₈–2 in long

NUMBER OF SPECIES:
8,000

*V*elvet ant

*S*awfly

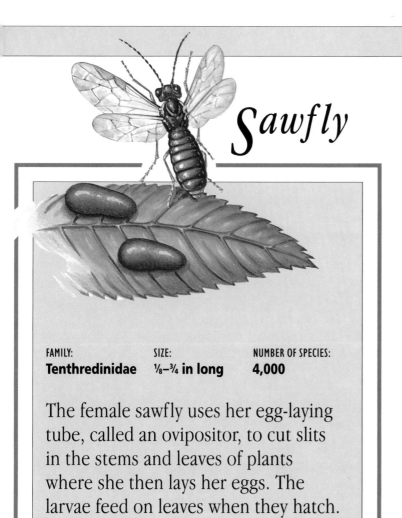

FAMILY:
Tenthredinidae

SIZE:
⅛–¾ in long

NUMBER OF SPECIES:
4,000

The female sawfly uses her egg-laying tube, called an ovipositor, to cut slits in the stems and leaves of plants where she then lays her eggs. The larvae feed on leaves when they hatch.

*I*chneumon *wasp*

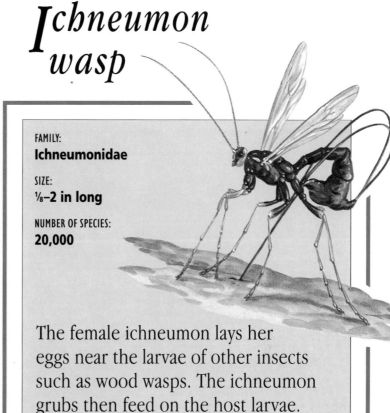

FAMILY:
Ichneumonidae

SIZE:
⅛–2 in long

NUMBER OF SPECIES:
20,000

The female ichneumon lays her eggs near the larvae of other insects such as wood wasps. The ichneumon grubs then feed on the host larvae.

Velvet ants are not ants at all but hairy wasps. Males have wings but females are wingless and have powerful stings. Females usually lay their eggs on the larvae of bees and wasps. When the velvet ant larva hatches, it eats its host.

FAMILY:
Mutillidae

SIZE:
¼–1 in long

NUMBER OF SPECIES:
5,000

*G*all wasp

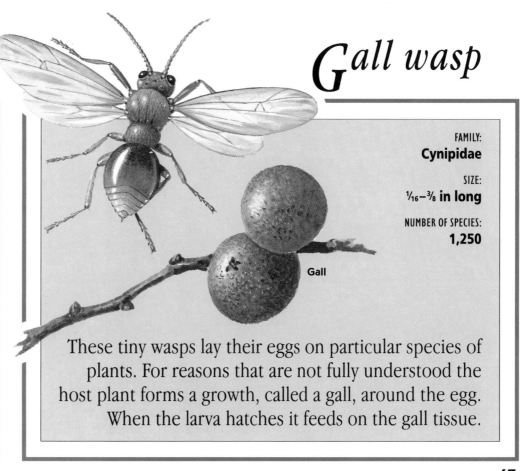

Gall

FAMILY:
Cynipidae

SIZE:
1/16–⅜ in long

NUMBER OF SPECIES:
1,250

These tiny wasps lay their eggs on particular species of plants. For reasons that are not fully understood the host plant forms a growth, called a gall, around the egg. When the larva hatches it feeds on the gall tissue.

*B*umblebee

Bumblebees are large, hairy insects, usually black in color with some yellow markings. In spring, queens, which are the only bumblebees to live through the winter, look for underground nest sites. Each queen collects pollen and nectar and makes food called beebread. Later, she lays eggs, and when the larvae hatch they feed on the beebread. These larvae become adult worker bees and they take over the work of the colony while the queen continues to lay eggs.

FAMILY:	SIZE:	NUMBER OF SPECIES:
Apidae	**⅛–1 in long**	**1,000**

*L*eafcutting bee

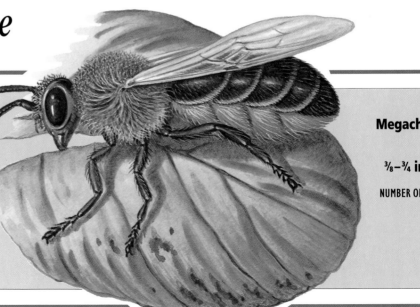

This bee gets its name from its habit of cutting circular pieces of leaves and flowers with its jaws. It uses the leaves to line larval cells in its tunnel nest, and an egg is then laid in each cell.

FAMILY:
Megachilidae

SIZE:
⅜–¾ in long

NUMBER OF SPECIES:
3,000

Orchid bee

FAMILY:
Apidae

SIZE:
⅛–1 in long

NUMBER OF SPECIES:
1,000

Most orchid bees live in tropical areas and are brightly colored. Males are attracted to orchid flowers for their nectar. They pollinate the flowers and collect scent, which may play a part in their mating rituals.

Plasterer bee

Plasterer bees nest in the ground. They line the tunnels with a secretion from glands in the abdomen. This dries to a clear, waterproof substance.

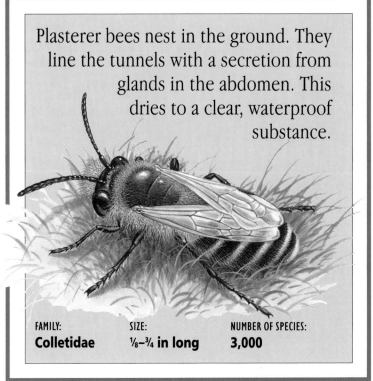

FAMILY:
Colletidae

SIZE:
⅛–¾ in long

NUMBER OF SPECIES:
3,000

Stingless bee

These bees cannot sting, but they have biting jaws. They live in colonies and make nests under the ground in tree trunks or even in part of a nest of a termite colony.

FAMILY:
Apidae

SIZE:
⅛–1 in long

NUMBER OF SPECIES:
1,000

Mining bee

FAMILY:
Andrenidae

SIZE:
⅛–¾ in long

NUMBER OF SPECIES:
4,000

Mining bees nest in long branching tunnels which they dig in the ground. Each bee digs its own nest but large numbers may live close together.

Spiders and scorpions

Arachnids, such as spiders and scorpions, are an ancient group of animals, dating back some 400 million years.

Few small creatures arouse such fear in people as spiders, yet nearly all are completely harmless. Only a few, such as the funnel-web spider, have a venomous bite that is dangerous to people. In fact, spiders do humans a service by keeping the insect population under control—all are hunters and they feed mostly on small insects. Some of the larger species, such as the tropical bird-eating spider, catch small animals and birds.

Spiders and their relatives, such as scorpions and mites, are arachnids, not insects. Arachnids have four pairs of legs and do not have wings or antennae. Although mites are the most abundant arachnids numerically, spiders have the most species. There are at least 35,000 known species of spiders in the world and many more are yet to be named. All spiders can make silk with the special glands at the end of the body, but not all build webs. Spiders use silk to line their burrows and some make silken traps that they hold between their legs to snare prey. Young spiders use long strands of silk as parachutes to fly away and find new territories.

Scorpions, too, have a fearsome reputation and some, such as the North African scorpion, do have stings that can be fatal to humans. Other arachnids are harmless, but whip scorpions spray an unpleasant liquid at attackers.

The hairy-legged wolf spider is a threatening sight as it hunts insects and other small creatures on the ground.

Harvestman

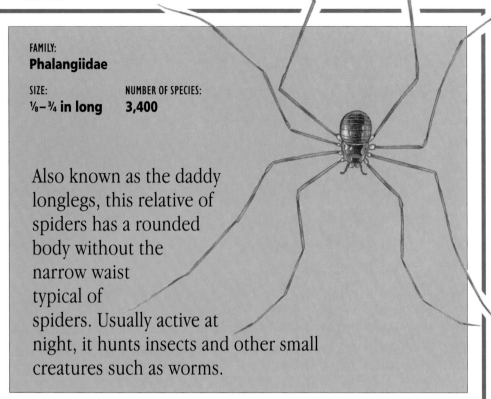

FAMILY:
Phalangiidae

SIZE:
⅛–¾ in long

NUMBER OF SPECIES:
3,400

Also known as the daddy longlegs, this relative of spiders has a rounded body without the narrow waist typical of spiders. Usually active at night, it hunts insects and other small creatures such as worms.

Scorpion

Armed with massive pincers for grasping its prey and a venomous stinger at the end of its body, the scorpion is a fierce hunter. It stays hidden during the day under stones or logs and comes out at night to catch insects and spiders.

FAMILY:
Buthidae

SIZE:
2–2¾ in long

NUMBER OF SPECIES:
700

Whip scorpion

Not a true scorpion, the whip scorpion has a long, thin tail and no stinger. It has four pairs of legs but uses the first pair as feelers. The whip scorpion's other common name is vinegaroon because it can spray an acidic, vinegary liquid from glands near the base of its tail when threatened.

FAMILY:
Thelyphonidae

SIZE:
5¾ in long including tail

NUMBER OF SPECIES:
100

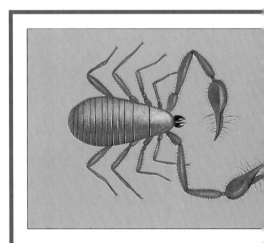

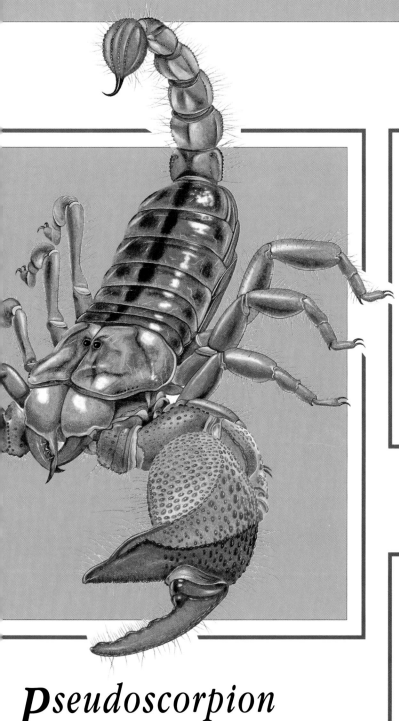

Tick

Ticks are parasites—they live by feeding on the blood of birds, mammals, and reptiles. They stay on the host for several days while feeding, attached by their strong mouthparts. Some species pass on diseases, such as Lyme disease, as they feed.

FAMILY:
Ixodidae

SIZE: NUMBER OF SPECIES:
¹⁄₁₆–¹⁄₈ in long   **650**

Wind scorpion

The wind scorpion, also known as the sunspider, is a fast-running hunter, common in desert areas. It has strong jaws and uses its pedipalps and front legs as feelers.

FAMILY:
Eremobatidae

SIZE: NUMBER OF SPECIES:
⁵⁄₈–1¾ in long   **900**

Pseudoscorpion

These soil-dwelling relatives of the scorpion have venom glands in their pedipalps, which they use when attacking prey such as insects. They do not have a stinger.

FAMILY: SIZE: NUMBER OF SPECIES:
Chernetidae **Up to ¼ in long**   **1,000**

FOCUS ON: *Orb weavers*

Very few creatures build traps to catch their prey. Among the best-known are the orb weaver spiders that build the webs most often seen in our houses and gardens. There are more than 2,500 species of these spiders living all over the world. They vary greatly in shape and size, ranging from tiny creatures only a fraction of an inch long to larger spiders with a body length of over an inch. Males are usually smaller than females.

Spiders build their webs with two types of silk that comes from glands at the end of the body. The silk is liquid when it comes out of the nozzlelike openings of small structures at the end of the abdomen, called spinnerets. One type hardens into extremely tough, nonsticky thread; the other type is sticky and used for the center of the web. Once the web is built, the spider waits near the center or hides out nearby, linked to the web by a signal thread. Through this the spider can sense any movement or disturbance in the web. Once a prey is caught in the sticky part of the web, the spider rushes over, bites it, and wraps it in strands of silk to prevent it from escaping.

Building a web

First, the orb weaver spider makes a framework of strong, nonsticky threads, firmly attached to surrounding plants or other supports. Spokes are added and the spider spins a widely spaced temporary spiral. With everything locked in place, the spider then moves inward, spinning the sticky spiral that will trap the prey and removing the temporary spiral.

Waiting on the web

This garden spider is lying in wait for an insect to blunder into its web and get caught on its sticky threads. The spider has extra clawlike structures on each foot that help it grip on to the dry lines of the web while avoiding the sticky spirals.

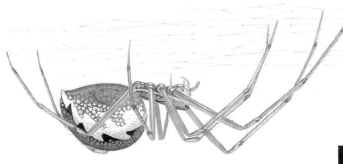

Sheet-web spider

Yet another kind of trap is woven by this spider. It makes a flat, sheetlike web and lies in wait beneath it. Above the web there are many threads holding it in place. When a prey hits these threads it falls down onto the sheet web, where it is grabbed by the spider from below.

Delicate trap

This glistening web of a sheet-web spider is ready to trap unwary insects.

Ogre-faced spider

This spider takes its web to the prey. It makes a small, but strong, net of very sticky threads in a framework of dry silk. Once the trap is made the spider hangs from a twig on silken lines, holding the net in its four front legs. When an insect comes near, the spider stretches the net wide so the prey flies into it and becomes entangled. The catch is then bundled up in the net and taken away to eat.

Crab spider

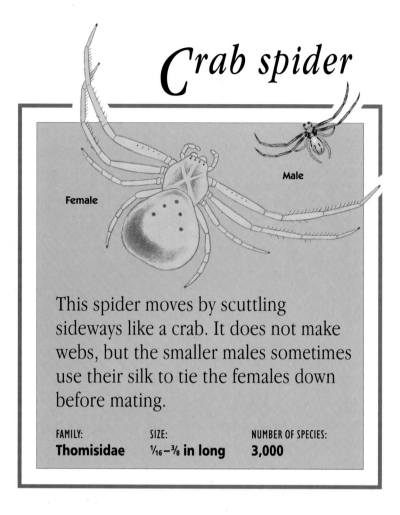

Female

Male

This spider moves by scuttling sideways like a crab. It does not make webs, but the smaller males sometimes use their silk to tie the females down before mating.

FAMILY:
Thomisidae

SIZE:
¹⁄₁₆–³⁄₈ in long

NUMBER OF SPECIES:
3,000

Jumping spider

Unlike most spiders, the jumping spider has good eyesight which helps it find prey. Once it has spotted something, the spider leaps onto its victim. Before jumping, it attaches a silk thread to the ground as a safety line along which it can return to its hideout.

FAMILY:
Salticidae

SIZE:
⅛–⅝ in long

NUMBER OF SPECIES:
4,000

Spitting spider

FAMILY:
Scytodidae

SIZE:
³⁄₈ in long

NUMBER OF SPECIES:
200

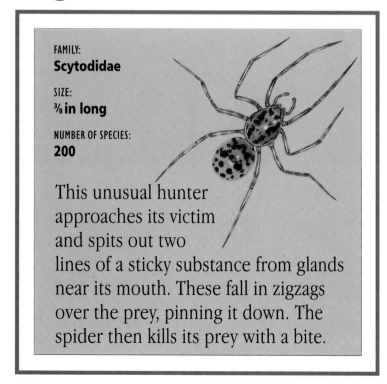

This unusual hunter approaches its victim and spits out two lines of a sticky substance from glands near its mouth. These fall in zigzags over the prey, pinning it down. The spider then kills its prey with a bite.

Trapdoor spider

The burrow of the trapdoor spider has a hinged lid at the top. The spider waits in its burrow until it senses the movement of prey overhead. It then pops out of the door, grabs the prey, and takes it back into its burrow.

FAMILY:
Ctenizidae

SIZE:
³⁄₈–2 in long

NUMBER OF SPECIES:
700

Black widow spider

FAMILY:
Theridiidae

SIZE:
Up to ½ in long

NUMBER OF SPECIES:
2,500

The female black widow has comblike bristles on her back legs that she uses to throw strands of silk over prey which gets caught in her web. She also has an extremely venomous bite, much more deadly than that of a rattlesnake. Males do not bite.

Wolf spider

Fast-moving hunters like their namesake, wolf spiders creep up on prey and seize it after a final speedy dash. Most do not make webs. Wolf spiders have good eyesight which helps them find prey.

FAMILY:	SIZE:	NUMBER OF SPECIES:
Lycosidae	**⅛–1½ in long**	**2,500**

Tarantula

The spiders in this family include some of the largest of all, with legs spanning more than 10 inches. Most hide during the day and come out at night to hunt insects and small creatures which they kill with a venomous bite.

FAMILY:	SIZE:	NUMBER OF SPECIES:
Theraphosidae	**Up to 3½ in**	**300**

Glossary

You may find it useful to know the meanings of these words when reading this book.

abdomen
The third part of an insect's body, behind the head and thorax.

antennae (singular, antenna)
A pair of slender, sensitive structures on an insect's head. Antennae help an insect to sense things in its environment by smell, taste, and touch.

cell
A six-sided compartment in the nest of a bee or wasp that is often used for the storage of food or eggs.

cephalothorax
The first part of a spider's body, comprising the head and thorax.

chelicerae (*singular*, chelicera)
Jaws at the front of the head of a spider or scorpion.

colony
A large group of insects that live together, usually in a nest. Ants, termites, and some wasps and bees live in colonies.

compound eye
An eye made up of many similar units, each with a tiny lens at its surface. Some insects also have simple eyes that have only one lens. Spiders have only simple eyes.

coxa
The first part of an insect's or arachnid's leg, nearest the body.

fangs
Pointed mouthparts, sometimes used to inject venom into prey.

femur
The third, often largest part of an insect's or arachnid's leg, between the trochanter and tibia.

gland
A part of the body that produces special substances, such as enzymes and poisons, which are passed to the outside of the body or into the blood. A gland in a scorpion, for example, makes the venom for its sting.

halteres
The hind wings of a fly which are reduced to a pair of small, knobbed structures. Halteres help the fly to maintain balance during flight.

host
An animal on or in which a parasite, such a a flea, lives and feeds.

larvae (*singular*, larva)
Young insects that look very different from the adult form. A caterpillar, for example, is the larva of a butterfly.

maggot
The wormlike larva of a fly.

mandibles
An insect's jaws, used for chewing.

naiad
Water-dwelling larva of an insect such as a dragonfly, mayfly, or stonefly. Naiads are also known as nymphs.

nectar
A sugary liquid made by plants that attracts insects. While an insect is feeding on nectar, it picks up pollen that it may then take on to the next flower. If this pollen reaches the female part of the plant, then that plant is fertilized and can produce seeds.

nymph
The young of an insect such as a grasshopper or dragonfly.

ovipositor
The egg-laying tube at the end of a female insect's abdomen.

parasite
A creature that lives and feeds on or inside another living creature. Fleas are parasites. They live in the fur or nests of other animals such as cats and dogs and feed on their blood.

pollen
Tiny grains made by the male parts of a flower. Pollen must reach the female parts of a flower so that seeds can form.

proboscis
Mouthparts specially adapted for sucking food such as nectar from flowers. The long mouthparts of a butterfly are called a proboscis.

pupa
The pupa is the stage in the lives of some kinds of insects when they change from larvae to adults. Butterflies, for example, pass through a pupal stage.

species
A particular type of animal. Members of the same species can mate and produce young that can have young themselves. Members of one species do not mate with members of another species.

spinnerets
The fine, jointed tubes at the end of a spider's abdomen. Silk for spinning a web comes out of the spider's body through the spinnerets.

tarsus
The fifth and last part of an insect's or arachnid's leg, attached to the tibia.

thorax
The second part of an insect's or arachnid's body, between the head and the abdomen. An insect's legs are attached to the thorax.

tibia
The fourth part of an insect's or arachnid's leg, between the femur and the tarsus.

trochanter
The second part of an insect's or arachnid's leg, between the coxa and femur.

venom
A liquid made by an insect or arachnid that is used to kill or paralyze prey.

Index

A
abdomen 9
ant 60
  army 62
  carpenter 62–3
  fire 62
  leafcutting 63
  velvet 66–7
anthrax 51
antlion 20, 22–3
aphid 28, 30
arachnids 11, 70–7

B
backswimmer 32
bedbug 28, 34
bee 9, 60
  bumble 68
  honey 9, 64–5
  leafcutting 68
  mining 69
  orchid 69
  plasterer 69
  stingless 69
bee sphinx moth 40
beetle 8, 10, 52
  carrion 55
  click 58
  darkling 58
  diving 55
  gold 52–3
  goliath 52, 54
  hercules 52
  jewel 55
  life cycle 10
  longhorn 58–9
  rove 54
  snout 58
  stag 56–7
  tiger 52, 55
  whirligig 54
biddy 27

body structure
  arachnid 11
  insect 8–10
boll weevil 58
booklice 35
bugs 28
  assassin 28, 34
  flag-footed 28–9
  giant water 28, 33
  life cycle 10
  plant 31
  water 32–3
butterfly 8, 10, 36
  birdwing 36, 42
  cabbage white 42
  copper 43
  lycaenid 36–7
  monarch 43
  morpho 43
  swallowtail 42

C
caddisfly 36
  large 39
carapace 11
caterpillar 36
cephalothorax 11
chelicerae 11
cicada 28, 30
cockchafer 9
cockroach 9, 12
  American 15
  German 14
  Madagascan hissing 15
cricket 12
  mole 9, 19
  true 19

D
daddy longlegs 72
damselfly 20, 26
  narrow-winged 26

darner 25
dragonfly 20, 24–5
  gomphid 25
  hairy 25

E
earwig 12
  common 14
  long-horned 14
  striped 14
exoskeleton 9, 10
eyes 9

F
firefly 59
flea 28
  cat 35
  chigoe 34
fly 44
  black 44, 46
  blow 51
  bot 51
  crane 46
  dance 46
  flower 47
  fruit 50
  horse 51
  house 8, 50
  hover 47
  robber 44, 50
  warble 51
froghopper 31

G
giant hornet 60–1
grasshopper 9, 12, 16–17
  cone-headed 16
  long-horned 16, 17
  short-horned 16, 17
grubs 56

H
halteres 44
harvestman 72
hawkmoth 40–1
head 9
hornet, giant 60–1
hornworm 40
hover fly 44–5, 47
Hymenoptera 60

I
inchworm 39

K
katydid 12–13, 16, 19

L
lacewing 10, 20
  green 23
ladybug 59
leaf insect 12, 18
legs
  arachnid 11
  insect 9, 10
Lepidoptera 36
lice *see* louse
locust 16, 18
looper 39
louse 28
  bark 35
  feather 35
  head 34
Lyme disease 73

M
malaria 49
mantids 20
mantis
  flower 20–1, 23
  praying 22
mantisfly 20, 23
mayfly 20, 26

midge 44, 47
  biting 46
mite 70
mosquito 8, 9, 44, 48–9
moth 9, 36
  atlas 38
  clothes 38
  cotton boll 39
  geometrid 39
  oleander sphinx 41
  poplar sphinx 41
  sphinx 40–1
  tiger 38–9
mouthparts 8, 9, 10
mud dauber 66

N
Neuroptera 20

O
ovipositor 19

P
pedipalps 11

pond skater 32
pseudoscorpion 72–3
psocid 35
punkies 46
pupa 36

R
royal jelly 64

S
sawfly 60, 67
scorpion 70, 72–3
sensory antennae 9
silverfish 12, 15
skimmer 26
snakefly 20, 22
spider 11, 70
  bird-eating 70
  black widow 77
  crab 76
  funnel-web 70
  hairy-legged wolf 70–1
  jumping 76
  ogre-faced 75

orb weaver 11, 74–5
  sheet-web 75
  spitting 76
  trapdoor 76
  wolf 77
spinnerets 74
stings 10, 66
stinkbug 28, 31
stonefly 20
  common 27
sunspider 73

T
tarantula 77
termite 60
  drywood 63
  snouted 63
thorax 9
tick 73
Toxorhynchites 49
treehopper 30
Trichoptera 36
tymbals 30

V
vinegaroon 70, 72

W
walkingstick 12, 18
wasp 60
  gall 67
  ichneumon 67
  yellow jacket 66
water beetle 9
water boatman 28, 32, 33
water measurer 32, 33
water scorpion 32
water stick insect 32
water strider 33
whip scorpion 70, 72
white-lined sphinx moth 40
wind scorpion 73
wings 9, 10
wireworm 58
woollybear 39

Acknowledgments

ILLUSTRATION CREDITS
Sandra Doyle/Wildlife Art: 30–31, 34–35
Bridget James/Wildlife Art: 38–39, 42–43
Alan Male: 8–9, 10–11, 54–55, 58–59, 72–73, 76–77
Colin Newman: 22–23, 26–27, 62–63, 66–67, 68–69
Steve Roberts/Wildlife Art: 14–15, 18–19, 46–47, 50–51
Michael Woods: 16–17, 24–25, 32–33, 40–41, 48–49, 56–57, 64–65, 74–75

PHOTOGRAPHIC CREDITS
1 Kjell B. Sandved/Oxford Scientific Films; 11 Michael Fogden/Oxford Scientific Films;
16 Belinda Wright/Oxford Scientific Films; 28–29 Michael Fogden/Oxford Scientific Films;
33 Colin Milkins/Oxford Scientific Films; 36–37 Phil Devries/Oxford Scientific Films;
41 A. G. Wells/Oxford Scientific Films; 44–45 Harold Taylor/Oxford Scientific Films;
49 London Scientific Films/Oxford Scientific Films; 52–53 Mills Tandy/Oxford Scientific Films;
56 K. G. Preston-Mafham/Premaphotos Wildlife; Harry Fox/Oxford Scientific Films;
64 David Thompson/Oxford Scientific Films; 70–71 J. A. L. Cooke/Oxford Scientific Films;
75 K. G. Preston-Mafham/Premaphotos Wildlife